Enchanted Evening

All this time Alma still couldn't speak. At least her hair was dry, she noticed in a daze, as he handed her into his car, the very same sporty Italian car she had seen him whipping around high school in, with Myrna Logan, back in real life. Now it was covered with thick, gray dust from the orchards.

Howard put the cake box on the floor, reached over and strapped her into the intricate seat belt. She would never be able to say a word. She would faint soon. He started the car, and they rushed along the now completely unfamiliar road. Maybe he never would say anything, either; just drive around and then take her home, and that would be all. It would be enough, more than enough, to keep her going the rest of her life. The wind blew the heavy smell of sulphured peaches in the window; the sun was going down and the leaves in the orchard were a dark, dark green. To her surprise, she heard herself speak. . . .

In Love And In Trouble

Laurel Trivelpiece

AN ARCHWAY PAPERBACK
POCKET BOOKS • NEW YORK

Another *Original* publication of POCKET BOOKS

POCKET BOOKS, a Simon & Schuster division of
GULF & WESTERN CORPORATION
1230 Avenue of the Americas, New York, N.Y. 10020

ISBN: 0-671-41274-4

First Pocket Books printing May, 1981

10 9 8 7 6 5 4 3 2 1

AN ARCHWAY PAPERBACK and ARCH are trademarks
of Simon & Schuster.

Printed in the U.S.A.

IL 7+

*This book
is for Mitch
and Matt*

one

By last period the heat filled up the hallways of Oaklon Union High School. The grass in the quad was worn and brown, even though the sprinklers were going. It had been a dry spring all over California, and here in the valley, the week before finals, it was a true scorcher.

Alma watched out of the corner of her eye as the rest of the junior English class filed slowly in. When at last Howard Babcock strolled through the door she let out her breath in relief.

They were finishing the term with "Song of Myself." As the hour came to an end, Miss Murdoch, a large woman with loose gray dimples on the backs of her plump hands, read out:

"Stop this day and night with me and you shall
    possess the origin of all poems,
You shall possess the good of the earth and sun . . ."

She looked up. "Who can tell us what Walt Whitman meant by these beautiful lines? Alma Ryder?"

Just her luck. She struggled to think of something, anything, acutely aware that Howard, in the last row,

1

his moccasined feet stretched out under the seat of the lucky girl in front of him, could hear the dumb thing she would say. At last she had to mutter, "I don't know."

Miss Murdoch smiled in her superior way. "Surely it's obvious? Whitman is celebrating the joys of good friends, communing with the good earth."

From the back of the room Howard's unmistakable laugh pealed out.

Miss Murdoch frowned, pretending not to hear. She didn't want a confrontation with her best student. Her favorite, too . . . With her extra-perception where Howard was concerned, Alma always saw and understood Miss Murdoch's blushes and fluttering hands when Howard sauntered up to her desk.

Now, as if summoned, Alma swiveled around, and Howard's bright eyes were on her, Alma. Deliberately, he winked—at her! The bell rang then, the class jostled out, but Alma sat, recovering her breath, the rich color flooding her face. It didn't matter that she still didn't understand the poem, or why he had laughed. She moved out to the hall in a haze.

He was leaning carelessly against the wall, as if waiting for her. Being up close to his body seemed to render her unable to move. He was so near she could smell his hair. He was going to speak to her. For a terrible moment she went giddy, as if she might faint, right there at his feet.

"Real live one, isn't she?" He grinned down at Alma, and her heart seemed pierced with sweetness.

He must mean Miss Murdoch. She spoke through a mist. "I guess I didn't get it. She didn't explain very well." The floor seemed to be buckling under her.

"You can say that again." But now he was looking over her head. Alma turned to see Myrna Logan, blond hair bouncing on her shoulders, skirt swirling around her tanned legs. He had been waiting for Myrna, of course.

"Sometime I'll clue you in." He smiled again, before moving off down the hall to meet Myrna.

Alma hurried blindly the other way, her ears singing. He had spoken to her. Howard Babcock had exchanged words with her! He had looked right at her as he spoke, smiled that wondrous smile for her alone. *Sometime I'll clue you in*. That could mean he planned to talk with her again. Of course it did.

Ever since she could remember, Alma had dreamed of just such an encounter. How many nights had she put herself to sleep, imagining Howard stopping her in the hall and speaking. Of course his words were different. *Meet me on the steps after class. There's something I must tell you*. And what he wanted to tell her was that he was in love with her, he had always been deeply in love with her. Nightly he fell asleep dreaming of her, as she did of him.

As far back as first grade she had had this hopeless fixation on him, although there were stretches of time when she was in grammar school, busy with Brownies and softball, that it had receded. But even then, it was there, simmering below the surface. This last year it had gotten much more intense, a pleasurable ache that haunted her always, a delicious, secret burden.

Howard's uncle ran Oaklon's only bank; his widowed mother was what was referred to as "comfortably fixed," so it was natural that he was at some distance from Alma. But, in the intercrossing ways of a small town, her lifelong best friend, Dilly, now dated a friend and teammate of Howard's. Occasionally, Dilly mentioned him, in passing, and Alma shuddered with emotion as she pretended his name meant nothing to her.

Dilly's parents were not only "nice people," in the Oaklon sense; they were also nice enough to have accepted Alma as Dilly's best friend, back in kindergarten. Over the years Alma had been included generously in the Meyer family as a matter of course. Everyone understood that it was a one-way thing: Dee, her mother, never expected to be invited to the Meyer home.

It made a difference that her father's sister had married the owner of Oakley, the big ranch between Oaklon and Delesto. Oakley gave her some standing, Alma knew, but on the other hand, her father's reputation wiped most of it out. "Goodtime Charlie" was pretty well known all over town, especially in the bars down on Fourth Street. And of course everyone also knew that Dee had been a Jenkins.

"Alma!" Dilly and Wilma, the third of their trio, came up to the locker they all shared. "You're standing there asleep, girl. We've got to call now; let's go." They had applied for summer jobs at the new MicMac hamburger place west of town. Dee had given Alma permission to go along. But she seemed to think that Alma didn't really mean it.

"You'll fink out, Alma, if we do get on," Dilly predicted. "Go out to your cousins at Oakley, like always."

Alma stacked her books in her pack. "Oh no. I'd love to stay in town and work. But it's up to my folks." She liked being able to group Dee and Charlie together that way, as if they could sit down and discuss something rationally, face to face, as other parents did, even if they were divorced. She'd have to corner Dee; she was the one who would really decide.

She said nothing about the miracle that had just hap-

4

pened, as she walked with the girls across the quad, heading for Dilly's to phone. She hugged it to herself. *Sometime I'll clue you in.* It was a sign; surely it was a sign. Something was going to happen between them, at last. She mustn't let herself be sent off to the country, not this summer.

two

THE MICMAC JOBS CAME THROUGH. BUT IT was late Saturday afternoon before Alma at last got Dee to sit still long enough to listen. Shouldn't she stay here in town and work this summer?

"But you always go to Oakley, baby." Dee watched her reflection in the mirror apply lip gloss. "What about your dad?"

"When Aunt Bernadine phoned this morning she said he had a job for the season," Alma answered mournfully. She peeled some old polish off her thumbnail. "He expects me out there, of course."

Aunt Bernadine had emphasized that, as she made plans a mile a minute for the summer of fun they would all have together as usual. Alma finally had managed to get in a word about the job she'd been offered.

"It's so nice for your dad, having you out here for the whole summer," Aunt Bernadine had gone right on as if she hadn't heard. Even she didn't suggest that Alma got much out of seeing him, but she knew duty when she saw it, and assumed Alma did, too. After all, she hadn't seen her father since Easter.

"Oh, I don't know what to do, Dee."

Her mother turned and gave her that hard, foxy

smile. She liked being called Dee. When she was little, Alma had called her "Mammy," until one surprising day Dee had snapped at her. "Mammy, Mammy. You aren't no little lamb, honey. I got a name, you know." Alma remembered that day well. It was fall, and the sycamore leaves were ankle deep on the sidewalk. They were moving out of the housing project on B Street, Dee had just landed her good job at the poultry testing plant, and the divorce had started. Charlie still came to see them, every Saturday night.

"How come Charlie isn't in here, urging you to come? It's all Bernadine. Of course she wants you back out there. Free help with those kids and the garden."

But Dee knew that wasn't so. Aunt Bernadine loved her, Alma thought, almost like an older, softer mother might, but that would be goofy to say out loud. Dee knew very well that Aunt Bernadine wanted her at the ranch simply so she could enjoy Alma's enjoying it all. The new kittens, the baby ducks, the little cousins—not so little anymore, Bobby was five now; last summer he'd wanted to swim with them in the irrigation ditch. No, nothing made Aunt Bernadine happier than to have Alma for the summer, one more to love and do for.

"He can't be drinking now, Dee, or he wouldn't have a job."

"Some job. Lifting cans off the belt. He'll never make it through peaches, anyway. First one laid off, we all know that." Dee spoke with undisguised relish, and she had reason for saying every one of those mean things about him.

It must have been genuine passion that had brought her parents together, and Alma had a dim memory of how it had been, lighting up their home, long, long ago. All these years later, feeling was still burning just as high as ever between them, only it had been turned

around and was hate. Now Charlie and Dee no longer
saw each other at all, not even a passing glance, if it
could be helped. But for a long time after they moved,
Charlie came in to stay Saturday night and Sunday.
It had always ended badly. Alma was relieved, really,
when he went off to Reno, where, she had heard Dee
say, he had lost all his money at the dice tables.

At first she had missed him terribly, but it was better
he wasn't there, trying to visit them, trying to sleep
lovingly with Dee; Alma assumed that was the reason
he followed her into the bedroom when he came. They
should have known by then that it wouldn't work, but
that burning hate-love, or whatever it was, kept them
at each other. She used to lie rigidly out on the sofa
bed that Dee had made up for her, fists clenched, waiting for the quarreling to start. Sometimes it was almost
morning before they began. . . .

Dee had boyfriends now; that's what she called them,
although they were pretty old. Dee could never look
old; she was one of those quick little women, hard as
a hummingbird; she had no soft edges to droop and
sag and wrinkle. Her name was really Samantha Dee,
which Alma had always thought an entrancing name,
but her mother never used it. The Dee part seemed
just right for such a small, bright person.

Her favorite boyfriend was coming over this evening.
Dee went with him a lot. They spent Sundays going up
to the foothills to watch the trail bike heats. Roger had
a hefty build and a big, red, bashful face. Dee said he
had his own dairy ranch, and she let him call her "hon"
and bring her ten-pound boxes of chocolates. He was
so shy he scarcely spoke, at least around Alma.

"Charlie is coming in this evening, then? I wish
Roger would step on it, so I can clear out first." But
Dee hadn't said what to do about MicMac's. She

seemed to think Alma would spend the summer out at Oakley as usual.

"Do you think I should take the job or what?"

"They'll all be disappointed if you don't go. And you never could get enough Oakley." Dee leaped to her feet. "I'm going to wear that new black and yellow I got at Langley's sale." Dee loved clothes. Back in the closet the garment bags and empty hangers muffled her voice. "Baby, you got to learn to make your own decisions."

From the bed Alma watched as she dressed. The new pantsuit fit as if colored on Dee's long-waisted little figure.

"There'll be lots of extra expense next year, with me graduating. I'd like to make some money on my own."

"Oh, money." Dee back-combed her top curls; she added two or three inches of height with her perky hairdo that would have made another woman look like a poodle dog. "I'll have the money for your graduation do's. We'll go up to the city to shop for your dress." Her eyes glistened. A shopping trip to San Francisco was Dee's idea of a real treat.

"Well, tell me, should I take the job?" Not for worlds, of course, would Alma mention wanting to stay in town because of Howard Babcock.

"Better find out what your father wants before you decide." Dee looked around for her red patent leather purse. "If he's going to be sober enough to notice, he'll want you out there with him."

That was true enough. And according to Bernadine, he hadn't been drinking; there had just been that one bad time at Easter. Alma took a deep breath; it wasn't easy to argue with Dee.

"But I'm old enough now to be making some money. Maybe I could go out to Oakley on my days off." She

had to be in town this summer . . . *I'll clue you in
sometime.* Oh, she was dreaming, as usual. Still, she
had heard that Myrna Logan was spending the summer
in art school in Mexico.

"Haven't we grown up all of a sudden." Dee turned
and, a rare gesture for her, she put her rough hand hard
on Alma's shoulder. "It's up to you. Time you learned
to decide, for yourself. But he *is* your father." Lonely
as this place was for her summers with Alma gone, Dee
never questioned that Charlie should have her then. A
girl ought to have access to her father, no matter if
he wasn't much anymore. Gratefully, Alma captured
her mother's hand, but the doorbell rang, and with one
last checking glance in the mirror, Dee trotted out to
Roger.

Alma wouldn't be lonely tonight, though, because
Charlie was coming in. One thing about Oakley: she
was never alone there; she couldn't get away by herself
for two minutes. When she had the chance, she'd slip
off to her special place, in the branches of the big white
fig tree. The great sun-splashed leaves concealed her
from view, while she read Aunt Bernadine's *Good
Housekeeping* magazines and ruined her appetite for
supper licking the pearly juice from the very tip of the
fig before splitting the soft, ripply flesh. But someone
would be calling her. Aunt Bernadine. Her cousins,
Bobby, Rhonda or Billy Jean. "Alma, where are you?
Let's go swimming." Or, "We're going to the store for
Frosties." "Come on over to the loading shed, see what
Ben found!" The smell of sulphur from Petroni's vine-
yards down the road weighed down the heat. The
Hinkels would arrive from Oakland, unpacking loaves
of sourdough bread, hugging and shouting; you could
never hear yourself think with the Hinkel cousins
around, laughing, teasing Aunt Bernadine. There was

room for all kinds of foolishness out at Oakley. Time itself stretched out. You could almost touch it, pure and hovering somehow, like the sunny green air above the plants Alma tended on the little porch there. Except for the time she had to spend with Charlie, the two of them trying to talk.

Luckily, last summer her father had worked the swing shift, and she didn't see much of him at all. It wasn't that she didn't want to see him; they just didn't have anything to talk about. Every summer she tried to connect the grinning, restless man with her long-ago Daddy, and sometimes, for a bewildering second, they would flicker and coincide.

She clicked on the television and sat down in the big chair. At her age, she ought to start making up her own mind, like Dee said. She was too wishy-washy, too dreamy. Wouldn't it be babyish to go back out to Oakley to play around all summer, especially if she ducked out on spending time with her father? Of course she should work at MicMac's. Dee would be pleased to see her "show a little spunk, for once," she'd probably say. And things went so much more pleasantly, if Dee were pleased. . . .

She jumped, but it wasn't the doorbell, it was the telephone. Charlie's voice was loud in her ear. "That you, Alma? How are you, honey? Listen, I want you to do me a favor. You come on down here."

"Where are you, Dad?" Her heart began to bang against her ribs. "I'm waiting for you here at the house, remember?"

"I want the boys to meet you. Come on down, honey."

She couldn't really tell, over the phone, whether or not he'd started drinking seriously. "Dad, I bet you're down there at the Beeline Bar!"

"Hell, girl, you sound like your aunt. Bernadine the bloodhound. I just dropped in to say hello to the boys. They want to meet my little girl. Nothing wrong in that, is there?"

"You've got to promise you'll come right home with me."

But promises meant nothing to him when he was drinking—she had no choice but to get down there as fast as she could.

When she saw him, waiting by the Beeline door, she had trouble finding the right voice. He was thinner than at Easter, his neck too skinny for his shirt collar, as he peered around the corner for her, jangling the loose change in his pockets. Seeing him was always hard, blurring the memory that still floated around in her mind. This was only an echo of the man who had been that Daddy she had been so crazy about. His good looks were marred now by a split lip that had never healed properly. He had gotten it in some forgotten fight.

She swallowed hard. "Hi, Dad." He hadn't had more than a beer or two, she estimated quickly. He still looked neat in his new wash pants, his shirt buttoned up to the neck, but parting above his belt buckle to show a white triangle of skin; he could never take the time to get that last button before jamming his shirt tails impatiently into his pants.

"Come on over here, sweetheart. I want you to meet the boys." His crippled smile always made her wince, until she got used to it again. The air was dank and smelled like rats. She didn't raise her eyes from the bartender's white, hairy fingers, swiping at the surface with a grimy rag.

"This is my daughter, Jerry."

12

The bartender didn't seem happy to see her.

"You give my girl here a ginger ale," Charlie went on, "and I'll have another beer."

The bartender looked straight at Alma, although he was speaking to Charlie. "You've had your beer, Charlie; you better take your daughter and run along." But it was Alma he was giving directions.

She could feel her face flaming, and she pulled at Charlie's elbow. "Come on, Dad, let's get out of here."

"What's the rush, darlin'?" He picked up the dice box. "Roll a round for the house, Jerry."

Oh, he had been drinking; now she could see the flushed trembling around the nostrils; his eyes were beginning to look puffy. But he hadn't reached the point where he couldn't turn back, if she could get him out of there.

"I'm going home, Dad. You want to come with me, talk about this summer, then come on. But I'm going, right now." She turned toward the door, hearing the bartender join in, "Go on now, Charlie. Take her home."

Alma knew her best bet was to keep on walking, toward the door. Sure enough, he followed her, and at the threshold he grabbed her arm roughly.

"Bernadine says you ain't sure you're coming out to the place this summer?" Of course, he had forgotten that last summer they had scarcely exchanged more than ten words! But, unwillingly, she had to remember things, like at breakfast. Every morning, under the shouts and gags of the others, Charlie had watched her, grinning to himself, letting his pancakes go cold.

"That's what I thought you were coming in tonight to talk about," she said reproachfully. How could she tell him she was considering taking a job in town? The mere thought of her not being at Oakley had almost touched off a drunk. A trapped, suffocated feeling began to fill her chest.

"Well, I want to know. Just want to know. Never want to pressure you, you rather be with her." He grinned that nervous grin.

The first thing to do was to get him away from the bar. "Come on home then, so we can talk about it." She almost ran up the street.

Charlie caught up and put his arm around her. "That's my girl. I figured you wouldn't pass up a chance to spend the summer with me and the folks." He sounded sober now, almost young and confident. Another flicker of that golden Daddy figure brushed through her mind. At least she had steered him away from what could very well have been the beginning of another bad bout.

But she'd have to go out to Oakley, as usual. She'd lost her chance already to make up her own mind. It wasn't right that she'd had to give in, be bundled off out there like a child. For a moment the anger was so hot in her that she kicked violently at a soft drink can some slob had dropped in the gutter; it banged and clattered across the empty street. Charlie grinned at her in a puzzled way.

They entered the house silently, and he sat down tentatively, as he always sat here, on the edge of the wing chair.

"Aunt Bernadine told me they took you on again at Pacific Peaches." She told herself she should be pleased he wanted her out there so much.

He shifted carefully in the chair. "Started Thursday. On the line; it ain't too bad. Where's your mother?" He said that last more loudly, knowing he had no right to inquire about her whereabouts. "Out with one of her fellas, I guess?" He gave Alma that sly look she hated. "Maybe you got a fella of your own now?"

She shook her head impatiently. Dee said that she was far too young to be interested in boys, brushing aside the fact that the other girls went out with them all the time. But Dee had said firmly that fifteen was too young. "There's plenty of time ahead for you. I'm not letting you rush into all that until you're ready." She made Alma refuse when a boy had asked her— only Harold Hansen, but still a boy—to the Christmas dance. Alma had been upset at the time, but it was awfully hard to argue with Dee, she got so mad. Alma had tried not to let it get her down. She had turned sixteen in May, and surely Dee would let her go the next time she was asked. But no one asked her to the Junior Prom, not even bespotted Harold Hansen. She didn't care. Howard Babcock's dangerously handsome face always swam into view at this point. She didn't need to be concerned with ordinary boys. She was waiting for something else. . . .

But Charlie worried about her lack of boyfriends. He wanted her to be a big social success, as well as at school; any B's on her report card thrilled him to pieces. It was depressing to know that he thought her accomplishments somehow made up for his failures.

To head off any more questions, she said quickly, "Dee's only got one boyfriend now, a really heavy one, though." Dee had a perfect right to marry again, and he'd just have to live with it. But she caught sight of the bewilderment—or was it pain?—in his eyes and was ashamed she'd told him. "How are things going at Oakley, Dad?" she asked hastily. "How's Aunt Selma and everybody?"

"Auntie's had a pretty good spring." Well into her eighties now, Great-aunt Selma had always been at

Oakley, in Aunt Bernadine's care. "But those kids—always full tilt about some foolishness or other. And old Ernie, he sets around reading his Bible, sniping at us all." He giggled and then stopped, reproachfully. "Bernadine and Ernie have been so good to me, honey. Bernadine saved my life here last spring. Saved my life."

Alma felt an ugliness choking up in her throat. Why did he have to make her think of last Easter's prolonged drunk! In and out of the county hospital, until Bernadine and Ernie caught up with him, carted him back to Oakley, and as soon as he was well enough, sent him off to his brother in Reno again. The kids at school must have heard about it, although no one had said anything—to her face. . . .

"I near died, I can tell you. Why, honey, if they hadn't taken me in again, I wouldn't be setting in this room today. Why, honey, I just hope that you'll be half the woman your aunt is."

She tried to swallow her anger. He was a fine one to talk. She just came out with it. "I was wondering, Dad, if it would be worth it, me coming out for the summer? I mean, with you working. Last summer, I didn't hardly get to see a thing of you." Her tongue felt big and thick. She should have started with the MicMac job.

"But I've got the day shift. Didn't Bernadine tell you? I'll be through every day by four; and even when the overtime starts, I'll be home for supper. We'll have lots of time together, don't you worry, darlin'." He picked at the threads of the bouclé slipcover. "The Hinkels are coming down in August. We'll have us a great summer out there." He was pleading now. For a moment the long-ago Daddy smiled out of his anxious, faded eyes.

"Sure, Dad." She got up, resigned. "You want some coffee? I could make some real coffee in the percolator?" She could hear Bernadine saying that, offering refreshments at Oakley to all comers. Suddenly, Alma couldn't wait to see her and all the rest of them. Her feelings swirled, confused with longing . . . and anger.

"Thanks, honey, but I don't want no coffee." Charlie smiled at her, much relieved, and then there was silence again. The business of the evening was settled, but he couldn't go yet. "Would you like to play a few hands of cards, honey?"

He always tried so hard, always in there straining. They couldn't be alone together a minute but he thought he had to generate some kind of fun for her.

"I don't think there's a deck in the house. Want to see what's on television?"

Together they went over the *TV Guide;* they could watch the rerun of *Hollywood Squares.* They sat solemnly together, enjoying this recess from talking, but the program was soon over. Alma offered coffee again; she always got as uptight as he did.

"No thanks, darlin'. School's out next week, ain't it. I'll come pick you up that Friday, after my shift."

"I'll have to do some things here in town first. Don't rush me!" Her cheeks burned with the effort to suppress her anger at being dragged out there, whether she wanted to go or not.

"Why, sure. Sure, honey. I just figured the summers go so fast."

"I said I'd come." She hesitated. "But there's this job I was offered, Dad, with the other girls. At the new MicMac's." At least she could just mention the job; she had a right to do that much.

"You wanted to take a job, not come to Oakley?"

"Well, I did think about it. But I'm coming, of

course." She didn't look up and flicked hurriedly through the *TV Guide* again. "I wish they'd show something halfway decent to watch."

"I always figured you had a real good time out at Oakley."

"I do, I do, Dad! But, well, I'd love to have a job for once." She warned herself to stop, but the words kept on coming. "We could use the money. I'm going to be graduating next year, you know."

"I'm makin' good wages. If your mother wasn't so damned stubborn . . ." It was one of the divorce's sorest points. All these years Dee would never take a penny from him for child support, although times were rare that he had it to offer.

"It's not just that. I'm sixteen, Dad, and well, the Hinkels and all that kidding around . . . last summer I got a little bored sometimes. I mean, I'm too big for new kittens."

But he wasn't listening, he was getting all worked up. "With overtime and all, some weeks I'll get checks for over two hundred dollars. I could give you all the money you'll ever need; you get your mother to see reason."

She might have known, she had known, how he would take it. "It's not the money. I just thought I'd like to take a job this summer. Maybe I could drive in from Oakley with you?" But that would never work. Cannery hours were unpredictable. Charlie would have to hang around town waiting for her sometimes. He couldn't take that; he'd start drinking. She looked at him and knew he knew it, too. That, and all the other words they couldn't say, flowed between them.

"Why sure, darlin'." Charlie got up. He moved purposely toward the door. "You got your own life to lead.

That Payless on the corner's still open. I'll run get us a deck of cards, sweetheart."

"We don't need to play cards. Listen, *Dragoon* is about to start; let's watch that."

But he kept on going.

"Wait, I'll come with you, Dad."

"No, no, you put that coffee on. I'll be right back." His broken lip stretched in a quick, somehow furtive, smile.

He was always so touchy, when he wasn't drinking. She walked with him to the door, waiting to hear herself speak, to tell him she was coming to Oakley, of course she was. She didn't care about any old job. But she couldn't make herself say it. She stood under the dim porch light, clutching his hand like a kid, but not saying it.

"You used to hang on to me like this when you was a little girl. And I'd come visit you. You'd hold on to my hand all the way out to the car, tellin' me you was having Jell-O, that red Jell-O you was so crazy about, for supper. You figured you might get me to stay, for that red Jell-O."

It flared in her mind so clearly. Every time he had left on Sunday, her Daddy, she was sure she was never going to see him again. The hot flood of tears choked her throat. "Jell-O, Jell-O!" She had shaken with deep sobs, bending over the porch steps, face burning with sorrow. Dee always blamed him bitterly. "Wears you out every time. All that crazy tearing around."

Dee might not let him come back—Alma had never dared express that terrible fear in words. Dee wouldn't let him, ever, ever come back to see her. She would bawl all through her bath, refuse to eat the red Jell-O, and in the end, Alma remembered, be spanked and sent to bed. "Stop it, now stop it—or I won't let him come back, upset you like this." It seemed, looking back, that every Sunday had ended in this black despair, sobbing herself to sleep. And every Monday morning it was all wiped away. The week had started out clean and fresh, with the promise of Daddy's weekend visit glimmering on the horizon.

"I'll put the coffee on, Dad; you hurry." It was all she could say, now, but when he came back she would reassure him that she definitely was coming for the summer. She stood there on the porch until he disappeared around the corner.

Until the first commercial she watched *Dragoon*. The coffee was done, and she started checking the clock every five minutes. At last she went to the door and looked down the street. She turned off the television and concentrated on watching the clock. An hour went by before the phone rang.

But it was Dee. "Did Charlie ever get there? We went by the Beeline, and I swear I saw him going in."

There seemed to be a whole crowd of emotions pushing up in Alma's throat. "He went out to buy a pack of cards, but he didn't come back. I guess it was him. Oh, it was him! Dee, I've made up my mind. I've decided for myself, like you said. I'm not going out there this summer."

"But you always had such a good time." Dee sounded more taken aback than pleased.

"No, I don't want to go! I want to take that job!" It didn't seem enough. "I always hated to leave you here all alone every summer anyway," she added, beginning to tremble. Something was going wrong.

There was a little silence before Dee answered, in a smoothed voice, "I could have managed. I always did. Never mind. Now don't wait up; you get on to bed."

Alma hung up slowly. Dee really wouldn't have

minded if she had been alone this summer. She was waiting for Alma to go, in fact. She said she wanted Alma to make up her own mind, but it wasn't so. She wanted Alma to decide to go; she had been counting on it . . . Dee and Roger, alone for the summer. She put it out of her mind, hurrying now to get ready for sleep as fast as she could, a great weariness spreading like relief through her. She got out a fresh nightie. Before morning Charlie would be lost; she hadn't saved him at all. It would be days, weeks maybe, before he would be in any shape to think about her.

Oakley was no place for her now; she had outgrown it: dear Aunt Bernadine flopping around in her shower sandals, the Hinkels and their jokes, the new kittens—all of it. The leaves of the big fig tree cupping around the dripping fruit, the amber wasps droning in the sun. In the evenings, Bobby, dimpled elbows like Aunt Bernadine's, pressed sleepily against her as they sat on the porch watching for the first star. Not this summer. She would be in town, within reach of Howard, she reminded herself; but for once, thinking of him didn't do a thing for her.

At the end of Charlie's drunk, he would be the first to say she shouldn't come near him; he always said that. He wasn't fit to wipe her shoes, and all the rest of it. Well, she was out of it now. The relief seemed to be soaking through to her very nerve ends. It was all settled. Dee was right to have refused his money, to have nothing to do with him. Dee—she didn't want to think about her, either.

Alma brushed her teeth and her hair an extra minute each, and was asleep as soon as the sheet was around her shoulders. An hour later she awoke, her heart brimming over. She wasn't going to Oakley. And Dee didn't want her to stay here.

She had forgotten to pull the shade, and the moonlight had hardened the shape of her clothes on the chair and was white and flat on Dee's empty bed. She wouldn't be home for hours; she was probably in another bed, with Roger. Alma thrashed over on her back. She had made up her own mind, and it had pleased no one.

three

THE FIRST FEW DAYS THEIR MANAGER, MR.
Gladburn, had them rushing around desperately, getting the place set up according to the MicMac master plan: the hamburger patties pressed to just the right thinness, the Styrofoam boxes lined up in exact stacks, relishes and catsup strategically arranged. But by the second week there hadn't been more than half a dozen customers a day, and time dragged endlessly for the girls.

Finally, their shift ended. The sun was still unmercifully hot out front, bouncing in red shimmers off the freshly painted building. Dilly's mother, who drove the three girls back and forth, was late again.

"It's that stupid Lance." Dilly detested her little brother. "He's probably conned her into picking him up at the pool." She put her hands to her nose and made a face. "Phewee! Whatever that is they put in that kinky MicMac sauce, I practically sterilized myself trying to get rid of it in the bath last night, but Mike said I still smelled just like a Big Mickburger."

Alma didn't bother to answer. It was amazing how tired one could get, just standing behind a counter, calculator and pad at the ready, waiting for someone

23

to come in and order something. She had too much time to think, especially about Charlie.

Of course, he had lost his job at the cannery. Aunt Bernadine had called up to say he was going to his brother in Reno again. "Your dad's feeling so low. It would have upset him more if you was out here. But the rest of us miss you so, honey."

"Oh, I'll be coming, Aunt Bernadine. Business is so lousy he's talking about laying us off for a while."

"Then you come right out! And try not to worry about your dad. He'll be all right."

Alma had hung up the phone, feeling ashamed that she wasn't worrying, as Aunt Bernadine assumed. What kind of daughter was she? She put aside these disturbing thoughts and turned to Wilma. "You try that strawberry-herb shampoo last night? Your hair looks just great."

The acknowledged beauty of their entire class, Wilma certainly had never needed to worry about attracting boys. She didn't have to worry about talking to them either; they were more than content just to be in her presence and watch her slow, beautiful smile as she listened to their bulling around.

She nodded and smiled back at Alma. "Jimmy and some dorky friend of his came over while I was still in the shower, rinsing. Mamma told them not to wait, but they hung around on the porch for hours. I was just too bushed; I went straight to bed with wet hair."

Alma tried to imagine herself in such a situation and failed immediately. Going peacefully off to sleep, while boys waited for her!

"Well, at last!" Dilly called out. The Meyer's old green car was unmistakable even in the clouds of dust blowing across the road. There were plowed peach orchards on either side. The MicMac people were really pioneering out from town this way.

"Oh dear, standing in this heat waiting for me." Dilly's mother parked, swung open the car door and poked back the hair falling in front of her eyes, all at the same time. "I promised your brother I'd pick him up at the pool. Well, how did it go today?" She had a long, freckled face—like a nice, friendly horse, Alma used to think.

"Great. We had three customers, total." Dilly, sitting up front, tossed her head, taffy-colored hair flying. "But old Gladburn had us whipping around as if the whole town was out there after his rotten burgers."

"Now, Dilly." Mrs. Meyer whirled the car expertly around. "It does you good to have your mind on something besides boys all day."

Alma and Wilma exchanged grins. All day long, working or lounging at the counter, Dilly talked nonstop about Mike. Mike, Mike.

"But listen, Alma. They're coming back tonight," Wilma said. "You come over for a while, too?"

Wilma, with all her boys to spare, had offered before to share with Alma. The first time, she had hurried eagerly home to ask Dee, because it wasn't like a date or anything, but Dee shook her head. "You're not having one thing to do with any boy until you're sixteen." Alma had hated the feelings that welled up in her then. She knew what went on when Dee was out all night. She had seen the lavender plastic disc full of birth control pills that Dee kept in her pantyhose drawer. And yet she treated Alma like a baby. Of course she didn't dare say any of that. . . . She couldn't talk back to Dee.

But now that she was sixteen . . . surely Dee would let her go. "I'll have to ask my mother. You know how she is." Her heart beat a little faster.

"She'll let you. You've had your birthday." Wilma smiled serenely. They had been best friends ever since ninth grade, when they had found themselves in Miss Quizenberry's gym class. A massive dislike for soccer had brought them together the first day. The boys were already clustered thickly around Wilma, the new girl in town. Sometimes Alma thought that she liked Wilma better than Dilly, although she and Dilly had been practically sisters since kindergarten.

"How's Dee this summer, Alma?" By virtue of the girls' long association, Mrs. Meyer and Dee had become inquiring-after friends, despite the gap between them. Mrs. Meyer was in the Delesto League of Women Voters, the Audubon Society; she even played bridge with Howard Babcock's mother. Of course, she knew all about Charlie's problem and always had, but she was far too kind-hearted to ever ask for news about him.

"Just terrific, Mrs. Meyer. She really likes having me at home for the summer, for once." Odd how she felt compelled to say that all the time. Well, in a way it was true. Dee didn't really seem to mind. Alma scrunched uncomfortably down in her corner.

"I bet you miss the family out at Oakley, though." Being part of Oakley gave Alma standing in Mrs. Meyer's eyes.

"If Mr. Gladburn does lay us off for a few days, I'll get to go out there." No reason not to go. Of course, she hadn't heard from Howard. And she did miss Oakley. Bobby—she felt a sudden tug in her heart. He must have grown since Easter, her last visit.

Wilma yawned and suggested, "You walk down about eight, when you get through supper."

"You hear that, Mamma. Wilma's fixing Alma up with one of her old boys and leaving me right out in the

26

cold." Dilly turned around on the front seat and bounced on her knees.

"You! I'm not about to get massacred for trying to break up your beautiful romance with Mike."

Dilly beamed at Wilma's lazy words, but her mother frowned. They knew Mrs. Meyer didn't like Dilly spending so much time with Mike, although he was from one of the town's nicest families, even a friend of Howard Babcock. Alma felt her heart dipping at just the thought of his name. Suddenly emboldened by the idea of the evening ahead, she asked, "Mike ever bring that buddy of his around, Howard Babcock?"

Still on her knees, Dilly doubled over on the seat. "Hoo, hoo! Come on, Alma. I'm not about to fix you up with *him*. You know he's always gone with Myrna." That was another thing. Howard even went with a girl from the class ahead; Myrna had graduated this year. She had been the Senior Queen—to the surprise of no one. A creamy blonde with a peach-colored tan, she looked good enough to eat.

"Anyway, from what Mike says, he's like 'mad, bad and dangerous to know.'"

The girls all knew what she meant. Miss Murdoch had made watching the TV show a class assignment, and that was what Caroline Lamb had written, thrillingly, in her diary after meeting Lord Byron at the ball.

Alma's heart began to jab faster. She was going to find out something new about Howard to add to her all too scanty store. She screwed up her courage again. "What's so mad and bad about being fantastically handsome, driving that car, and being a real brain in the bargain?" She could have added being on the basketball team, in the Honor Society (she heard he never went to the meetings) but everyone knew that, just as they knew about Myrna and him.

Mrs. Meyer swerved the car around a dog lazing in the middle of Frontage Road. "He has real problems, that boy. Ever since his father died."

"Listen." Dilly bounced on the seat again, holding on to her glasses. "He writes poetry; he told Mike, but he never showed it to him. And he was into speed, but he told Mike he's all through with that, and listen,"—she lowered her voice, solemnly—"he tried to commit suicide once. He told Mike. No one realizes his mother drinks like a fish—" her voice came to a stop, confused; she sat abruptly back around to the front. The back of her neck was turning red.

Mrs. Meyer rushed in. "In spite of all your gossip, Dilly, I think he's a nice boy. More than once I've seen him driving old Mrs. Bunden home with her groceries. What his mother does is not his fault. He's not responsible in any way for his parents' shortcomings," she added pointedly. Oh, everyone in town had always known about Charlie.

Alma hurried to get out of the car before any of this exciting hoard of new knowledge could escape her. His mother drank, too—talk about bonds! Someday, ah, someday . . .

Wilma's voice broke in on her dream. "About eight, then. I don't know who this guy is, and neither did Mamma. You'll just have to take potluck."

Alma nodded, almost absently. The information about Howard was foremost in her mind. She floated up the front steps, forgetting she was tired. Howard was one of the few kids in their class who would go on to college, Stanford or some such place, not just Delesto Junior College, where Dilly and Wilma would enroll. Not Alma, although her teachers urged her to consider it. Dutifully, she had repeated the urging to Dee.

"I could get a better job after taking business courses at junior college."

But her mother had shaken her head. "That secretarial course you're taking there at the high school is first-rate, everyone says so."

What was Alma to say? She would rather work with little kids, be a kindergarten teacher, than in an office; but that would mean expensive years at college. No, she could never even suggest such a thing to Dee, who had gone on firmly, "Be a foolish waste. I've been at it a long, long time, honcy, to keep us going, and I wouldn't have had it any other way. But when you graduate, it's time for you to get started on a good job. Two paychecks should make quite a difference around here."

Funny how teachers always took it for granted that parents were as hot on college as they were. When her advisor talked to her about it, she seemed to think all Alma had to do was to decide to go. It would have been as hopeless to try to explain to her how Dee saw the situation as it was the other way around.

When she walked in, Dee, who got home from her job by four, had a fresh apron around her little waist and was cleaning the kitchen cupboards.

"Where all this stuff comes from. You think Bernadine could use these peanut butter jars for pickles? Ohhh! Kill it, kill it! Ugh! Nasty thing." Dee had big, homely hands for her size; she grabbed a rolling pin and smashed down the daddy longlegs. Alma couldn't say anything, she couldn't criticize Dee, although she herself felt compelled to lift spiders and the worms she found in the lettuce onto bits of paper and transport them outside. A long-ago scene spun into her mind. Sometimes she was sure it hadn't really happened. A wet spring and the sidewalk in front of that little house

on B Street, where they had all lived together before
the divorce, was sparkling with slimy snail trails. Dee,
coming in with the groceries, stopping and systemati-
cally crunching the snails under her high, sharp-heeled
shoes. Charlie shot out of the house, cursing, pushing
her over on the grass. "Leave them alone! Leave them
alone!" Weeping, he carried the snails one by one,
crushed or whole, to the safety of the hedge. He was
drunk, of course. If it happened at all.

Dee looked up, that penetrating look that went right
through her. "How'd it go today, baby? You look
worn out."

Alma ran a long drink of water. "It seems like I've
been standing at that counter waiting for orders for
about two years. He's going to lay us off if we don't
get some customers. Dee . . . there's something I want
to ask you." It was silly to get so flustered. She had a
right to ask. Sudden thoughts of rebellion rose up in
her before she could smother them. If Dee made her
stay home tonight, she'd complain to Charlie. Dumb!
He was in Reno. And anyway she couldn't bear to
think of them fighting over her.

"What? You got such a funny look on your face."

"I was just wondering if you were going out or anything tonight," she mumbled.

Dee sprang to her feet and started lining up the dusty
peanut butter jars in the sink. "No. I told Roger, 'Let's
skip tonight; I need to do my hair and nails.' Besides, I
thought it would be nice just to sit around and watch
TV with you. I was out so late last night."

Alma couldn't look her in the eye. They both knew
she'd been with Roger all night, but she'd never come
right out and say so to Alma. Dee had two sets of
rules: one for her and one for Alma. It was so unfair.
But knowing her mother was planning to stay in to-

night made it all the harder to ask. Maybe she should just let it go. She wouldn't. She heard herself saying, "Dee, I want to go down to Wilma's. There's these," —she swallowed, shaken by her own boldness—"boys coming over, and she wants me to meet this friend of Jimmy's. I'm sixteen now, Dee." She ran it all together.

There was a silence, and then Dee gave a little laugh and turned away from her jars. "Now let me think. Your blue pants need washing, and there's something wrong with those you got at Carter's; I've got to fix them."

"You mean I can go!" Alma jumped up happily. "Oh, Dee, thanks. Oh wow!"

"You *are* sixteen. Roger said the next time you asked, I should let you go. He said I shouldn't be so uptight about you."

Alma blinked, a little taken aback to discover that Roger, who only grinned bashfully at her, could actually talk—he and Dee talked her over. It was a new idea; she put it aside for later thought. "Oh, Dee, what shall I wear?" She beamed happily down on her mother. Alma had always wanted to be tiny and cute like Dee, but she was already two inches taller and more rounded. Secretly, she thought her face was too round—her cheeks were like a chipmunk's—but she had Dee's dark eyes: small, but Russian black. They made a nice contrast, she knew, with her light, penny-brown hair, which she wore parted in the middle and draped back over her ears. Luckily, she had washed it last night, so it was glinty in the light. The girls always said she had really neat dark eyebrows.

Her heart fluttered up light as a bubble. "I can't wear my new dress. I mean, we're just going to sit

31

around, I guess. Play some records. We might go downtown for a Frostie or something."

"Hoo, look at you. He just better be a nice boy, that's all." But Dee didn't sound worried. One thing about her, once she made up her mind, that was that. She didn't let doubts and fears creep in. "I'll iron the white jeans while you take your bath. You wear your tank top with them."

Dee knew, of course. She always knew just what Alma should wear. Other girls might have more "background," as Mrs. Meyer would say, but with Dee's taste and sewing skills, none of them was better dressed. Sometimes it flashed through Alma's mind that she was almost excessively color coordinated, just a shade *too* put together.

After supper, Dee suggested she dampen and re-blow her hair. She was really throwing herself into this, as if it made her feel better about going out all the time herself.

At ten minutes to eight Alma's heart dropped, and her hands began to shake.

"Hold still, I can't reach that side." Dee wielded the hair dryer like a pro. "What's the matter? It's coming out just beautiful."

Alma twisted her hands behind her. "Dee, I don't know what to talk about."

"Why don't you just let Wilma and the boys talk this time. They'll talk."

"Wilma won't. She doesn't have to; she just sits there and smiles. And what if the boys don't say anything? Or Wilma and Jimmy go off?"

"Don't you worry, baby, you look so pretty. You'll have fun."

"What about you, Mother?" Mother, where had that come from? She could feel Dee frown and hurried on, hoping she would let it pass. "What are you going to do here by yourself, Dee?"

"I got multiple choice, that's for sure. If I don't run out of steam, I'll finish up the cupboards. I've got to go through my drawers and clean out the closet, too. I want to put out some things I can't wear anymore—for Billy Jean, next time you go." Billy Jean, her Oakley cousin, was as short as Dee, but chunky. Whether she could get in to them or not, she loved Dee's discards. Usually there was a suitcase full of them. So far this summer, her suitcase had just been gathering dust under the bed.

"If we get laid off for a few days, I'll be going pretty soon."

"When? This weekend?" Dee said, a little too eagerly. "Me and Roger'll run you out any time. Just say the word."

"Mr. Gladburn said he'd let us know tomorrow." It made Alma feel suddenly lonely, the way Dee and Roger were so hot to get her out to Oakley the first possible moment.

"Okay, baby." Dee got up briskly to hold the door for her. "Now remember, tomorrow is a work day, so don't be late." She would be waiting up, Alma knew, snug in her pink quilted robe, with the television on, just the little table lamp burning.

She made herself smile brightly. "See you." She ran down the steps, aware that Dee was watching through the screen door. She trotted down the sidewalk, as if leaving her anxiety behind. But when she got in sight of the Santos' yellow stucco house, her steps dragged. What if she messed it up?

They were all on the front porch, Wilma and the two boys. She recognized Jimmy Ghilotti, even if he was partly hidden by the honeysuckle vine; he played

football and had such big shoulders. The other boy—
she couldn't make herself look. Jimmy could have
brought a teammate.

Wilma was laughing huskily at something the other
boy had said.

"Hi there." Alma stood uncertainly on the bottom
step. The three of them were laughing louder; they
hadn't heard her coming. She had to clear her throat
and say it again, louder. "Hi there."

"Hi there, Wilma." Why did she keep saying the
same stupid thing over and over? "This is how you
recoup from the big Micks?" As she said it, she saw
that it didn't make any sense, and sounded moronic
besides.

But Wilma smiled her warm, all's-well smile. "Sit
down here beside me. I want you to meet a friend of
Jimmy's. Nelson Parks. He's new in town, from Berkeley, and you better not believe a thing he says."

Wilma was really the sweetest girl in the world. Re-
stored, Alma took a good look at the boy lolling on
the steps on the other side of Wilma, but he was so
deep in the vines she couldn't see much. "Hi. Welcome
to Oaklon. Will you be going to Oaklon Union High
next fall with the rest of us?" That wasn't exactly bril-
liant, but she had to say something.

The boy laughed, wheezed really, in a hollow way,
as if for his ears alone. "No. No, I don't think Oaklon
Union High is in the cards for this lad. Ah, no." He
turned abruptly back to Wilma. "So what do you say?
We could make a bundle. I'll come get you tomorrow,
take you over to my studio."

"Studio. Man, you can really sling it. What you've
got, baby, is a closet in your father's garage, that's
what you've got. A crummy darkroom. Where you get
this studio bull!" Jimmy sounded really riled.

"Nelson, I'm not going anywhere tomorrow but straight to my job. Alma and me are working at the new MicMac's."

"What a town. A real live, genuine beauty like you drudging away in a MicMac grease pit. What kind of a perverted dump is this place? Don't they realize they've got the next big star in their midst? Baby, I'm taking you away from all this." He deepened his voice, exaggerating the vowels as if he fancied he was imitating someone in an old movie.

"Nelson's a photographer, Alma," Wilma explained. "That's his hobby."

"Hobby!" For the first time Nelson turned to Alma. "I've had a pic published in the *Berkeley Weekly Enquirer,* that's all. I'm a pro, baby. And with a subject like the little fox here, the two of us could make it big. I hear *Playboy* pleading now. Centerfold layout, all the way."

Poor Jimmy looked as if he could kick himself for bringing this loudmouth along. The boy moved out from under the vines, and Alma could see that he wore huge glasses on his plump face and had an unusually big bald forehead. He didn't look to be very tall, either.

"Man, I feel sorry for you, man." Jimmy gave an unconvincing laugh. "Trying to lure the chicks with that creaky come-on about photographing them."

"He's just putting me on, Jimmy." Wilma smiled soothingly. "Hey, let's walk over to the park and see who's playing tennis." When she got up, the others followed obediently. Jimmy captured her hand and hurried her on ahead.

Nelson was taller than Alma, but he was heavy. His chest and belly made one curve. Well, she needed to practice; it should be easy with this boy.

"Where'd you live before you came here, Nelson?"

To her surprise, he didn't answer. Just grinned, leered rather, at Wilma's back up ahead.

"You think he's in there, with your friend?"

"Listen, what are you saying?" She couldn't believe her ears.

"I wouldn't take his word for it, no way. Those two getting it on?"

Alma stopped walking. "That's a dumb thing to ask me."

"So don't have a cardiac. All I'm saying is she's out of that poor turkey's class, way out of his class." He laughed that breathless, colorless laugh under his words.

"I thought you were a friend of Jimmy's," she said stiffly.

"My folks, his folks, the poor jock himself—for years they've thought we were. Don't tell him, hey?"

She felt more confused than ever. They walked along silently. "I'm sorry Oaklon doesn't come up to your standards," she said sarcastically. "I guess it's not much, compared to Berkeley."

"Too right. Listen, you see that movie at the Larkin? The only movie in town? You do yourself a favor, man, take in that flic."

They were beginning to have a conversation. Eagerly, she answered, "You liked 'The Possessor'? My mother told me it was X-rated. How'd you get in?"

"There are ways, little one, there are ways. Wow, that was great. He guns each one down a different way, see." The rest of the way to the park he outlined, in some detail, all the gory scenes from the movie, gesturing largely with his fat hands. He wore two wristwatches. Alma made a point of pretending to listen. Practice, she told herself, practice. He wasn't much; she could imagine the post mortem with Wilma, the two of them doubling up over what a big-mouthed fat boy he was, but for now she would use him for practice. She needed to practice, not just dream how it was going to be. *Sometime I'll clue you in.* If Howard Babcock ever did call her, any experience she could rack up now would be all to the good. It flashed through her mind that it was possible Howard might never call. She was letting year after year slip by in a dream . . . she put that thought down at once.

Nelson was clearly impossible; she couldn't care less whether he liked her or not. But it would be okay if he would go for her a little, take her out a few times, call her on the phone. That way she would know all the ropes when Howard . . . It will happen, she told herself. As Nelson babbled on, she remembered that day in English class. She saw again that lively face, the blue eyes winking right at her. He knew she was there that day. She wondered again why he had laughed at Whitman's love poem. It just wasn't possible that she could go on being so obsessed with him, if it weren't going to be a mutual thing, someday.

Sometimes she wondered if everyone else could see how extraordinary, how, in fact, godlike (she wouldn't want to say that out loud) Howard was? There were certainly better athletes in school, and bigger brains, even other brainy athletes; he wasn't the only A student on the basketball team. But it was more than that; it was the special atmosphere he had around him, a sort of "don't touch me," almost a royal aura. When he smiled, it was of such surpassing sweetness. The stirring of air when he happened to jostle by her in the hall brought a glow to her cheeks, making her forget whatever friends with her were chattering about.

Ever since she had been a little girl, she had taken her mind off the quarrels that raged above her, and then later, after Charlie left, the loneliness, by telling herself stories. She used to spend entrancing hours, acting out fairy tales in her head while she sat on the sofa waiting for Dee to get home. She was Snow White or Sleeping Beauty, the enchanted princess waiting for the prince to come and release her. More and more all her longing for the prince had been distilled into the desire, if that was the right word, for Howard. It must be desire, this melting that turned her to liquid inside when she saw him. Did it happen like that for other people, or only for her? All she knew was that if he ever came to her, say, in study hall, and beckoned, she would get up at once. She could see it all so clearly, laying down her ball-point pen, putting her math and English books neatly aside, checking her hair and following him straight out of the room. Wherever he wanted her to go, she would have no choice but to follow. And he didn't even begin to suspect that he had this terrible power over her. She had to shiver when she thought of it, impressed, and sometimes even a little scared at her own feelings.

And now she had learned that his mother drank, too. What could it be but another sign? Sooner or later Howard was going to come to her, recognizing that she belonged to him, and he to her. . . .

But the business at hand was this Nelson, such as he was. When he finally stopped narrating the movie, she spoke with confidence. "You're not like the boys around here, are you? What do you like to do, when you're not seeing X-rated movies?"

He liked that, she could tell, feeling him becoming aware of her, a girl beside him. "In due time, little one, all will be revealed. Listen, what's your name?"

"You hadn't been so busy back there trying to dazzle Wilma, you might have heard. My name's Alma."

"Alma? *Alma?* Ah, well, I've got me own troubles.

Listen, you're the fox's buddy, right? So tell me, Jimmy got the inside track there, like he claims?"

"You better ask Wilma." She paused, curious, and after all, everyone liked to talk about himself. "What troubles, Nelson, these troubles you have?"

"What with being dragged to this godforsaken excuse of a hick town, what other troubles would I need? Listen, I had a sweet setup in Berkeley. I was getting all I could handle."

"This isn't such a bad place; give it a chance." Alma hesitated. She didn't want to hear about what he was "getting"; he was lying, anyway. But she said, placatingly, "It *is* a shame, having to leave all your girl friends behind."

He eyed her thoughtfully. "Want to try out for a spot in the lineup? I can't promise anything, but there just might be something."

She wished he'd stop talking like that, so phony; but, taking a deep breath, she tried to return the ball. "I'll have to think about it." She was almost sure that was how Dilly would have answered, and of course Wilma didn't ever have to say a thing—just smile. She cast about for another subject, but nothing came to mind.

"Yeah? You wouldn't try to bull me now, would you?" Nelson gave her a long, neutral look. "Listen, you want to make my team, how come you walk like that?"

"Like how?" At least she had gotten his mind off Wilma; that was something. "How should I walk?"

"You're scrunching along against that wall, six feet away, like I'm going to spring on you. I don't have to fight for it, you know. Relax."

He was making fun of her. "I don't know what you're talking about."

"Baby, I would just bet you don't. Listen, you can

level with me." He grinned at her in a swaggering way. "You are, aren't you?"

"I'm what?" She straightened her lips, lifted her chin. He just wasn't going to get to her.

"Untouched by human hands. The only virgin in town. Am I right? Yeah boy, I can spot 'em every time."

She turned her flaming face from him and walked faster. They were almost to the tennis courts. Up ahead, on the other side of the bright, bougainvillaea-draped gate, she could see Wilma and Jimmy embracing. A sudden longing for Oakley enveloped her like a net. Long, warm evenings like this they spent out on the porch behind the honeysuckle. Bernadine made pitcher after pitcher of lemonade from their own sweet lemons; Bobby stretched over the doorsill, fast asleep. Why wasn't she out there where she belonged, instead of with this big-mouthed slob? She broke into a run, determined to catch up with Wilma and Jimmy, whether they liked it or not.

"Hey, what's the rush? You mad about something?"

She wouldn't turn around—but suddenly she did, and the words poured out. "Who do you think you are? A fatso like you; listen, you'll never get to first base with a girl like Wilma in your whole life, don't you know that!" She was amazed to hear herself saying these hateful things, amazed that the hot blood coursing through her veins was such a pleasure. She stopped and glared at him, fists clenched. Inside she was reeling with pleasure at her own ferocity.

"Yeah, how about that." And that's all he said.

Deflated, bewildered, Alma walked in silence beside him. Had she actually said all that? The silence went on. She couldn't stand it. "Hey, I'm sorry I sounded off so much." She cleared her throat. "You're not fat, Nelson. Husky, you know?" Alma glanced over at him, wanting him to understand. "It's just that you made fun of me. You hurt my feelings," she added in a low voice.

"I didn't go to do that. I get crazy sometimes. Keep blowing off." Nelson scuffed his feet. His voice was altogether different now, almost pleading.

"Okay. Let's forget it." She was glad that was over with, and they could catch up with the others. She couldn't help admiring the way she had spoken up—she, Alma Ryder—and put the old city boy in his place. "We're friends, okay?"

"Friends." When they came in through the dark park entrance, Nelson called out, "Hey you guys. Wait up for foxie and me!"

"Well, well, Cinderella, about time you showed up." Dee was curled up in the big chair waiting. "Click that TV off. So, what was the boy like?"

Alma flopped down on the sofa and then bounced upright again. "His folks just moved here from Berkeley. He's not handsome or anything, but he's very funny, a smart talker. Dee, we had more fun." The early part of the evening could just be forgotten.

"Well, good! What did you do?"

"Just fooled around. Took a walk to the park and watched the tennis. Then we went downtown and had Cokes at Meely's; a lot of kids from school were there." Secretly, she was glad that Howard hadn't shown up. She would love for him to see her out with a boy, but not with someone as fat as Nelson. She put the thought down guiltily. "Then we went back to Wilma's and played some crazy new game her little sisters have, and that's all. Just fooled around." She yawned luxuriously.

"Did he ask you out?" Dee got up to wind the clock,

calling from the kitchen, "Maybe you won't go out to Oakley now?" She sounded suddenly worried, as if she and Roger were really looking forward to having the place all to themselves.

Alma tried not to think about that. "He didn't ask me out, but he did say for me to come over sometime and see where he does his photography; he's got this darkroom."

"Darkroom. Uh-huh. I know what he's after. You stay out of there, baby."

"It's not like that." She had almost forgotten the early part of the evening, and that didn't count now, anyway. "He's not after anything."

"Baby, they're always after one thing. Let me tell you."

Alma's resentment rose, but she bit it back. *You ought to know, you ought to know. You're after sex, too, and what's more you get it, all the time*. It was sneaky, and dumb, too, the way she tried to make Alma think it was so great to be a virgin.

Alma undressed in silence, pretending to be too sleepy to talk any more. Her last thought was a hope that Mr. Gladburn would close down the place tomorrow, so she could go right out to Oakley.

four

MR. GLADBURN DID DECIDE, AS HE PUT IT, "TO fall back and regroup." They would close down for a week. "But we'll get 'em on the Fourth of July weekend, troops." A skinny little guy with long, kinky hair that spurted out in all directions, he loved to talk as if the girls were his private army.

Right after supper, Dee and Roger drove her out to Oakley, not staying for her rapturous welcome. But before the next day was over, Alma realized the whole feel of the ranch had changed, now that she was just a visitor.

Monday turned out to be blistering hot; like a hostess, Billy Jean suggested they go swimming in the big irrigation ditch. Rhonda, the twelve-year-old, was away, but they took Bobby, both girls mindful of Aunt Bernadine's warning to "watch him now, girls, every single second." It wasn't that the big ditch was so very deep, although it was way over Bobby's head, and it did run fast. The danger was that the sides were steep and paved smooth; there were only certain places where you could find handholds to get in and out of the water.

"He shouldn't swim here at all." Billy Jean tossed her shirt in the weeds. She was in a sulky mood. Her father still wouldn't let her go out with boys, and she was a full year older than Alma. Compared to Ernie, Dee was an enlightened parent.

"Mamma makes me take him everywhere." Billy Jean shook out her jeans. "You watch yourself now."

"I'm not going to drown," Bobby shrilled, his eyes round as blue and white marbles. "I can swim just as good as you, Billy Jean. I can go all across the pool at school under water." He stood with locked knees, like Bernadine did, so his thighs bulged out fat as drumsticks.

"We're not in a pool here, you remember that, tiger." Wind was blowing through the peach orchards, and the leaves shimmered white. The dust burned the soles of their bare feet. Gingerly, they slid down the concrete sides of the ditch. Around the bend they could hear faint whooping and splashing—probably the Petroni pickers, rinsing off the peach fuzz. Alma and Billy Jean exchanged faint smiles. Past summers they had made a big thing of giggling over this neighborhood crew, teasing each other about going down to meet them, but this time it was different. She and Billy Jean were not a team, were not "the girls" this summer, even though they were together.

"Hurry up, Alma!" Bobby was already dog-paddling across, but Alma didn't try to catch him. She couldn't move very fast in her old suit. When she tried it on, all faded out from last year's sun, she found it was a good size too small, almost slicing her in two. It would have to do until she had a chance to go shopping. The water stretched it out so she could move around; she really didn't swim. She splashed, and floated on her back. The sun made interlocking rings of light behind her closed lids.

Without looking she pulled herself up on the rock

that jutted out on the other side; after all these years, she knew where it would be. Billy Jean towed Bobby back and forth and then left him to practice her crawl. Both girls ignored the faraway, masculine shouts from around the bend. Alma floated back across, passing Bobby, now paddling like a puppy, midway. She found the fingerholds on that side, climbed out and folded some of the long brown weeds for a place to spread her towel. The sun was like warm oil on her legs. Most summers by this time she was as brown as Bobby. She stretched and dozed.

Billy Jean's wet head appeared above the ditch. "Bobby up there with you? Where's Bobby?" In the sudden silence they could hear the ditch water slapping the concrete.

As if in slow motion Alma got to her feet. It seemed to take forever, that simple act—and then time speeded up. They were running up and down the path by the ditch, not feeling the thorns in their feet. "If he isn't playing right here . . ." They rushed back to the ditch. But only lonely little swells of water were rushing by. . . .

"Bobby. Bobby!" Cold waters were closing over Alma's head—she would never, never surface again. . . .

"He's in there! Down there, see, see!" "Caught under the pipes. Dive, dive!" The helpless, criminal feeling of not being able to dive like Billy Jean, to get to him! Through the cloudy water she could see Bobby's leg's draped around some pipes at the bottom. Billy Jean dived and snatched; the sun blasted on the surface of the water as she came up gasping and spurting—without him. She must go get help—the pickers around the bend—it was her voice shouting, louder, louder! Billy Jean dived again—Bobby, Bobby! Then a great, hurling bird shot by her into the water, to the bottom and came up with Bobby, slamming him chest first on to the hard ground. Water gushed like a dirty fountain from his mouth, and his wonderful live bleats filled the air. Billy Jean fell on the ground beside him, hugging and gasping, while Alma backed weeping into the rescuer's arms, feeling a hard chest moving up and down, hearing the harsh breathing. She drew back at once, but it had all happened before. . . .

Howard Babcock. He gripped her by the forearms. "You mustn't faint; hey, don't do that. Why, I know you!"

She came back to herself in a rush, all too aware of how she must look, crowded into her faded, frumpy suit. She turned, swinging her hair in front of her, not daring to look at that glowing chest where she had actually leaned. She gestured clumsily to the pair on the ground.

"Bobby's my cousin—so is Billy Jean. Bobby's the one you saved."

He grinned at her, and his eyes were so blue she couldn't look away. His hair curled up around his strong neck.

"You saved his life." The air around her seemed on fire.

"I suppose you could put it that way." He kept on looking at her. "Maybe you better take him home." Billy Jean wrapped the whimpering Bobby in Alma's towel, and Howard carried him back out to the pickup.

"You spending the summer out here, Alma?"

If she took care not to look at him, not to bear straight on the impact of his face, she could talk, she found. "I'm just visiting at Oakley for a few days. I've got a job in town, at the new MicMac's. What—what are you doing out here?"

46

"I'm on Petroni's crew for the season." He leaned into the pickup window. "So we're neighbors."

"I live at Oakley," Billy Jean said shortly. She was somehow the extra one. Now Bobby sat up between the girls and brushed back his towel. "You want a kitten? We got a black one and a gray striped and a white one. You can have which one you want. And with black spots!"

"Bobby, he just saved your life. Isn't that enough? Don't go trying to lay one of your kittens on him!" Now Alma could permit herself to look at Howard. But her legs trembled; she knew he was seeing her bareness, really exposed by that horrible, fadey old suit.

Billy Jean let out the clutch with a roar. Sticking her head back out of the window, she shouted to Howard, "Thanks, thanks! Some of us will be around to thank you." She nearly hit the road marker getting back on Oakdale Avenue. "Wow, he's cool. And you know him! Oh, Bobby, Bobby. Alma, we'll have to tell, and Dad will kill me."

Sobered, Alma had to think of that. Uncle Ernie was awfully strict, and they were horribly in the wrong. He was going to come down on them hard, especially on poor Billy Jean. He seemed to have it in for her all the time anyway.

Aunt Bernadine, of course, understood. She fell on the now dry Bobby and sobbed with happiness. In no time at all she had him in the bath, washing off the last remnants of danger, her face aglow with the wonder of him alive and well. She didn't say a word of reproach to the girls—just cautioned them as usual to be sure to wash the ditch water out of their hair. It wasn't exactly put into words, but everyone understood that the matter wouldn't be referred on to Uncle Ernie, unless of course Bobby said something.

"Thank the Lord, Auntie's still asleep. She naps so much these days," Aunt Bernadine said, happily toweling Bobby's hair.

The color had returned to Billy Jean's face, and she went back upstairs to the macrame hanging she was making. It was decided that she would drive her mother, and a big coconut cake, over to Petroni's the next day, to thank Howard formally.

Alma hung around the kitchen, unable as yet to function on her own. It was really too hot to have the oven on, but Aunt Bernadine had the cake in the works already. "All right, honey, you want to help, beat these egg whites."

"Funny. Here we are cooking away, just like nothing ever happened."

"My, yes. Can't ever stop for what might have been; just thank our lucky stars and go on. Oh, that blessed, blessed boy."

Alma couldn't tell if she meant Bobby or Howard. Aunt Bernadine had such pretty brown coloring, echoing the beige and red roses printed all over her sleeveless shift, her usual summer garb that hid her too-full figure from view.

Alma put her eggbeater down and gave her a big hug. "It's so great to be back out here, Aunt Bernadine. I really miss you all so much." Howard—Bobby—she felt she was about to explode with too much emotion.

"That reminds me. This was in the mailbox." She reached in her pocket, brushing off a raisin stuck to one corner of the postcard. "Charlie's always so good about remembering to write."

The glorious roar of the encounter at the ditch bank receded. Alma took the card, written in soft, faded pencil.

Dear Sister:
    Just to let you know I got here o.k. Leonard
met me at the bus. He's putting on a new roof
this summer, glad to have me here to give him
a hand. I'm sure sorry for all the trouble I put
you to. Tell Ernie I will send the money he
gave me for my ticket. I hope Alma gets out
real often. Tell her and Aunt Selma and all
the kids hello.

                            Love, Charlie.

"Writes a real nice card." Aunt Bernadine put it back
in her pocket. "Remembers us all. You got a letter off
to him yet?"

Alma involved herself with chipping at the worn
spots in the plastic table cover. "Not yet. Well, I didn't
have a second to myself, with that job. Aunt Bernadine,
I never know what to say to him."

"Honey, all he wants to hear is that you're not holding it against him, that little spell, and that you're okay,
having a good summer. That's all he wants to know."

Alma felt little and spiteful, thinking how she just
plain hadn't written to him. "I'll get a letter off tonight,
I really will. Did Bobby go to sleep?"

"He's in there, singing to himself. By suppertime,
he'll have forgotten all about it."

No, Aunt Bernadine wasn't going to give them away
to Uncle Ernie. She was always on the job to keep him
smoothed down. The least little thing could set him off,
scolding and laying down the law, quoting Scripture at
them. Not for the first time, Alma wondered how two
as unlike as big, pillowy Aunt Bernadine and a hard
little wasp of a man like Uncle Ernie, so into the Bible
that he had no time for his children or anything, ever

got together in the first place. Once they had, Alma could see how they kept going. It was all Aunt Bernadine's doing. She smoothed and arranged, keeping from him the children's little sins, sweeping troubles under the surface. Just her mild suggestion, "I might have to tell your father, if you do that," was enough to bring them up short, Alma very definitely included.

At supper Uncle Ernie piled his plate with potatoes and corn beef. "Pass me a biscuit, Billy Jean. You girls go swimming? That crew at Petroni's go down to that ditch. I hope you stayed away from them."

Bobby looked up, as if remembering, and Aunt Bernadine and Alma rushed in at the same time. "We got a card from Charlie, honey!" "Bobby, how many kittens did you say Old Blue had? Can I name one? Samantha?"

Uncle Ernie frowned, waving his fork at Alma. "Don't get him going on them kittens. Ben don't want him down to the barns all the time worrying the stock." Ben was his longtime foreman, the only person at Oakley that Uncle Ernie never criticized. Now he yanked his head at Aunt Bernadine. "Can't you see to it this girl has a swimming outfit that covers her?"

Alma turned red. He must have watched them drive off this afternoon; it was mean the way he always noticed things.

"You let them go around half naked, flaunting themselves like they was harlots." Uncle Ernie actually used words like that. Harlots. His knife clanked against his plate as he attacked his corn beef.

"Now, honey," Aunt Bernadine soothed, "The girls were just swimming out here in the ditch, no one around . . . You don't want to speak so hard to Alma, the first time she's been with us all summer."

"For her own good," Uncle Ernie answered testily. "Ain't it our duty to guide her into chastity?"

"My stars, yes. Who wants berry cobbler?"

The girls leaped up to clear away, not daring to let their eyes meet. In the kitchen Billy Jean minced up and down in front of the stove, throwing out her stocky hips, twirling an imaginary mesh bag. "How about it, honey? Twenty dollars a trick?" They doubled up with laughter, and it took awhile to get themselves together enough to go in with the cobbler. Alma, smothering a last giggle as she dug into her piece, realized happily that now they were "the girls" again, she and Billy Jean. The happiness of this never to be forgotten day was complete.

After supper Uncle Ernie left for some parish business. Aunt Bernadine went dreamily on with frosting the cake, and Billy Jean went across the road to show her macrame to the Bradshaw girls. Before she left, she had put on a stack of old dance records. The music echoed through the house, as if it were a manifestation of the joy rocking through Alma.

Now that she'd calmed down, she would have liked to escape to her fig tree and go over the afternoon, every delicious detail, but Bobby begged her to read to him. They did all of his favorite stories; it was almost dark when she got up to turn over the stack of records. Bobby scampered for a World Book to top off the stories. Methodically, from A to Z, he had them read to him.

"What have you got tonight? R. Okay." The music swayed on; between records they could hear Bernadine out in the kitchen moving slowly around. Alma felt steeped in the peace of Oakley. She couldn't believe she wasn't there for the long, endless summer, belonging to them all again. Tomorrow she would go along when they delivered the cake to Howard. . . . Howard out here; it was more than she had ever dared dream. She would quit her job and come back to Oakley as soon as she could.

"Look at these, Alma." Full-page color pictures showed the growth of a fetus in the mother's womb. "Like the kittens." Bobby breathed right into the pages, not wanting to miss a single marvelous detail. "See, their eyes are closed, too. Which one do you choose?"

"They're all the same baby. The pictures just show how it grows from month to month." In silence they looked them over. The babies didn't look like kittens. Their unborn faces were square and sorrowful, with little oriental folded eyes.

"It'll be nice, won't it, Alma. A little baby growing on a stem like that inside you?" Bobby, wrapped up in his corduroy robe—a gesture toward the afternoon's danger, for it was still warm—looked up trustingly.

At that moment the bell at the back door rang, and they both waited as Aunt Bernadine scuffed over to answer it. There was a bell at the front door, too, but it never rang. Everyone just naturally came around to the kitchen at Oakley.

five

BOBBY BROKE FROM HER LAP AND RAN TO THE kitchen; there was a babble of voices. Aunt Bernadine's rose higher. "Why, I made this cake for you! Oh, there's no possible way we can thank you enough. It's just a blessing that you were there, and such a fine swimmer."

Alma sank back into her chair, deprived of breath and sense. The air was shimmering around her again.

Bernadine called, "Alma! Come on out here." As if in a dream, she slowly removed the towel from her hair. She was, she would be, in her oldest, tackiest shirt, and there were grease spots on her shorts. Her legs and feet were pink from the afternoon sun. She padded obediently out to the kitchen. Howard Babcock, standing in Aunt Bernadine's kitchen! Bobby was tugging at his hand, chirping away.

"You can show him the kitties some other time, Bobby," Aunt Bernadine chided. "Young man, you just draw up that chair and let me cut you a piece of cake. I sure hope you like coconut."

None of it seemed to be real. Aunt Bernadine, waddling around in her shift and shower sandals, the adoring light on her face, the eagerness with which she cut and placed a towering piece of cake in front of Howard, who was smiling—it must be a dream.

"Best cake I ever tasted, Mrs. Pollard," he announced after the first bite. "Maybe we can make a regular thing of this, Bobby."

Not understanding, Aunt Bernadine laughed and hurried to the refrigerator to get him some ginger ale.

"Aren't the rest of you having any?" Howard was looking right at Alma.

As if hypnotized, she came closer to the table, shaking her head. When she realized she was standing there staring at him, like Bobby was, she quickly pulled out a chair and sat down, but still watched him eat, as if fascinated by the shape and number of his fingers. She couldn't say a word.

Howard pushed back his chair when he finished. "That was a beautiful experience, Mrs. Pollard. I just dropped by to see if the boy was okay, but if I'd known you had a cake like that on hand . . . Alma,"—he turned to her abruptly—"would you like to come out for a ride?"

Aunt Bernadine sat down and folded Bobby onto her lap, nodding happily at the invitation. "But my land, look at you. Have another piece of cake, Howard, while Alma gets tidied up a little."

"Couldn't possibly manage another crumb. She looks okay; we're just going to ride around." He started for the door. There was nothing for Alma to do but go with him, over Bobby's protests about kittens and Bernadine's cries about the cake. They had to wait while she found a box and string for it.

All this time Alma still couldn't speak. At least her hair was dry, she noticed in a daze, as he handed her into his car—the very same sporty Italian car she had seen him whipping around high school in, with Myrna

Logan, back in real life. Now it was covered with thick, gray dust from the orchards.

Howard put the cake box on the floor, reached over and strapped her into the intricate seat belt. She would never be able to say a word. She would faint soon. He started the car, and they rushed along the now completely unfamiliar road. Maybe he never would say anything, either; just drive around and then take her home, and that would be all. It would be enough, more than enough, to keep her going the rest of her life. The wind blew the heavy smell of sulphured peaches in through the window; the sun was going down, and the leaves in the orchard were a dark, dark green. To her surprise, she heard herself speak.

"You never worked for Petroni before, did you?" She studied his profile hungrily.

"I'm having lots of new experiences this year." He kept on looking straight ahead. "Mrs. Petroni is some sort of relative of ours. My mother's away for the summer, so my dear uncle fixed it up for me to come out here to slave in the peaches. My mother's, uh, visiting some, uh, friends in Denver."

As clearly as if he had shouted it aloud, she knew that his mother was not visiting friends; she was in one of those drying-out hospitals. How could she tell him that she understood, that it didn't matter, his having an alcoholic parent; in fact, it was a marvelous bond between them. She did manage to say, tentatively, "My father's away this summer, too."

Howard didn't answer. The miles sped by; they were way over beyond the river now. He looked at her and smiled; it seemed to spread through her like rings of light. She studied her lap.

"We're all so thankful for what you did, Howard. If anything had happened to Bobby. . . ! I'll bet my aunt won't let him go swimming again until he's about thirty years old."

Howard said nothing and drove on; they went down narrow, two lane roads, and country lanes that seemed lost among towering orchards. Alma sat entranced; to speak again might break the spell.

After what seemed like hours, Howard pulled the car deep into someone's walnut orchard. It was quite dark now. When he turned off the ignition, they couldn't hear anything but the lonely little swish of the leaves moving in the night breeze. He looked at her almost with surprise, as if he had forgotten she was beside him. "There was nothing to what I did. I heard you girls screaming, and it was all a reflex. I always wondered how I'd do in a situation like that. I'm glad I had a chance to find out I'd be okay."

"Okay? You were a real hero, Howard." She raised her eyes to his face, glimmering in the dark, and looked hastily down again.

There was another silence.

Then he said, softly, "Hey. You. Know why I came by?"

Alma kept her eyes on her unseen, tightly bent knuckles. "You wanted to see if Bobby was all right." Her voice was strangely husky.

"I knew that kid was all right the minute I fished him out. I came to see you." He tilted his head back against the seat and laughed. "I came to see you because you have absolutely gorgeous legs. Alma Ryder, of all people." He sat up suddenly and looked at her, challenging her. "How about that?"

"Oh." She felt a silly urge to look down, check them out herself. They moved whitely in front of her in the dark. She made a sudden decision, the right decision, she realized later. She wouldn't try to fake this, to come

56

on as if she had been around. She would play it straight.
"Do I? I didn't know that. I mean, I know they're all
right, not deformed or anything." Her voice tightened.
"But no one ever told me before that I have beautiful
legs." She felt very childish, but calm. No way in the
world could she compete with a sophisticate like Myrna
Logan, and she would be a fool to try. "I'm awfully
glad you think so."

"Hey." He put his perfect hand on her bare thigh;
she started and trembled violently, but made no move.
"Well."

As if he didn't know quite what to do next, Howard
took his hand away and moved back to his side of the
seat. "I remembered you from English class. Miss
Murdoch, silly old turkey."

She hid her shock. "One day you laughed at something she said about a poem. Do you remember? That
poem of Whitman's? I always wondered what was so
funny."

To her astonishment he recited the lines in that beautiful, somehow vulnerable, voice:

"Stop this day and night with me and you shall
        possess the origin of all poems,
You shall possess the good of the earth and
    sun . . ."

Unaccountable emotions swirled inside her as she sat
listening. When he finished, she could hear the crickets
in the ditch. At last she said, "That's a celebration of
friendship . . . and ecology, or something . . . according
to Miss Murdoch. But you laughed." Whatever it was
leaped higher and brighter in her veins.

"Friendship. Poor old ninny. But how in the hell
could she know."

"Know what?" Alma could hardly speak.

He was looking at her almost sadly. "That poem isn't about friendship. It's about love, physical love. Sex. You know?"

She shook her head, for some reason close to tears. "No, I don't know. Like Miss Murdoch. I don't know anything."

Howard slid back. His hand was on her thigh again, and the burning was branching throughout her body. "I don't know anything, about anything," she whispered again.

As if under the same spell, he whispered, too. "Do you want me to show you? Shall I show you, Alma Ryder?"

It was pitch dark now, but he saw her nod, and he reached over for her hand. She started shaking again, and he smiled as if he understood, that it was all right for her to be made so that she couldn't help trembling when he touched her. Through the dark she still saw that smile.

He helped her out of the car, and, as if in a trance, she waited while he rummaged in the trunk for a blanket. Her lungs and heart had ceased operations. Time itself was standing still. Whatever happened, she must go along with it, as if they were in one of her own unfolding dreams. But she thought suddenly of Dee. She'd be so shocked, so outraged, if she could see her "baby" now! But it was her turn to find out just what it was like, this secret act Dee pretended was to be avoided. She was soon going to know. The stars were thick in the sky, but it was almost the end of June; that was when the sky was closest, and stars very big and near. Now they were whirring and wheeling like demented moths above them.

"Sure it's okay?" Howard whispered. When she

nodded, he tipped her face up to his, and she saw the mystery glinting in his eyes. Before his lips touched hers, she felt his warm breath, like a flowering all over her face. They sank together on to the blanket.

Alma stirred, strangely cramped, parted from Howard's warm body. They had been laying apart like that for what seemed a long time. He had been the one to roll away; he lay staring at the sky.

"Howard." She could say his name like that—tenderly—now. She wondered when they would have to go back to the car, and then he would take her home. "Oh, Howard. It was wonderful." Her voice sounded very phony. It was crazy to be crying.

"So how come the tears?" He rolled near again and brushed them from her cheeks. "You're a flaky girl, lying there crying as if you'd been seduced or something." He sounded a little ashamed. "Why didn't you stop me?" Gently he lay his cheek on hers. "But you liked?"

"I said so, didn't I?" She was beginning to feel easier, as if they were friends. They must be friends now. Soon she would have to sit up and arrange her clothes, believe what had happened. Overwhelmed as she had been, it also had been painful. But she said again, stubbornly, "It was wonderful. You were."

Howard pulled a battered pack of cigarettes out of his pocket. "Wonderful, huh. Yeah, I should be."

She had to think of Myrna then as she quickly buttoned her shirt. Of course they had broken up, Myrna and Howard. People broke up all the time, and now he must want to go with her. Didn't he? She sat without words again, still stunned, thinking of the amazing thing he had done to her.

"I better take you home. My skinflint relative will have us all out in the trees by dawn tomorrow."

"Well, when the fruit's ready," she said automatically. That's how it was during the peach season; everyone around Oaklon knew that, except Howard, evidently. Impulsively, she bent over him and then drew back, too shy to initiate a kiss on her own.

"Hey, why didn't you stop me." He blew smoke out, looking at her all the time. The moon was out now, and they could see each other clearly. "I never expected you to turn on like that."

Her heart filled with pleasure at the tenderness in his voice. Now if she could just stay cool, no pushing, no coming on.

"What's Myrna doing this summer?" She was aghast at her words, but it was too late to recall them.

Howard didn't seem to think she had said anything amiss. "Mexico. Conned her dad into sending her to some art school down there. She hasn't written once. And Mother's been packed off . . . Mother's away, and so here I am, you see, abandoned and deserted." He threw away his cigarette and got up abruptly, putting down a hand to pull her to her feet. "Left on my own. I guess that's my apology or alibi. Or something." He folded the blanket and started back to the car barefoot, his moccasins in his hand.

"You don't need to apologize." He didn't answer. She walked in front, dismayed by the soreness when she moved, bewildered by what he had just said. How different the sky looked now.

"Hey, wait up." He threw a comradely arm around her shoulder. Would he want to see her again soon? If only she were staying out here all summer, as usual. He probably didn't know where she lived in town. She couldn't tell him until he asked. How everything had changed. It was clear, crystal clear, that the Howard Babcock she had appropriated for her dreams had vanished, like the supernatural being she had thought he was, gone forever, and here stood an all too real person who had been her partner on that blanket, making love. Someone who stopped and swore.

"Wait up a minute. Damned thorn in my foot." He leaned his weight on her shoulder and dug for the thorn. "Hold it, you're not steady enough. What are you, some frail, feminine type or something?"

"Go ahead, break my collar bone." The mirage she had mooned after had never existed. She had been playing games, making up a private dream. But this was actually happening. This boy cursing the thorn in his foot, leaning, playfully, intimately, on her shoulder, was a stranger. His finely molded lips weren't godlike, they were heartbreakingly human. A great new weight seemed to descend on her, and it was very real. The incredible event back there on the blanket, this flood of feeling. She wasn't ready for it. But she would have to handle it now, this love affair; she was committed to him now.

As if she had summoned it up with that thought, he began to speak of Myrna. "I'm supposed to be eating my heart out this summer, you see. Of course she didn't know Mother would be going away—" He stopped as if it had occurred to him that he shouldn't be talking about Myrna just now. "Well. You see now what I mean about Miss Murdoch missing the point? Aren't you glad I came along to demonstrate, clear up the mysteries, the ambiguities, in that poem?"

Ambiguities. He knew so much; he wrote poetry himself, she remembered. She tried to match his playful words. "I can't thank you enough. I'll think of you, Howard, every time I assign Whitman to my class."

"What will you tell them the lines mean, Miss Ryder?"

She cleared her throat and said as lightly as she could, "I'll give them some starry-eyed stuff about how the earth moves, or something." She knew she had said the right thing because Howard laughed as if relieved.

"You tell 'em, teach."

He whistled and sang under his breath all the way back to Oakley, almost as if he were alone in the car. The moon was so bright one could have read a newspaper. The big fig tree cast a deep inky shadow over the old pump house.

He reached over and opened the car door for her, but then, as if remembering something, quickly got out and came around to her side. They walked to the door, his arm around her shoulders. He kissed her, lightly.

"You're quite a girl, Alma." That seemed to be all he was going to say about what had happened, or was it good-bye? She stood inside the screen door and watched until his lights vanished down the road before she turned to grope her way to the bathroom.

She could hear Uncle Ernie snoring in the bedroom down the hall he shared with Aunt Bernadine, and she dared not run water for a bath and chance waking him. She cleaned up as best she could and crept upstairs to her own little room. Everyone in the house had been sleeping sweetly away while this miracle had happened. It hadn't been at all like she had imagined—rather painful, too. How really physical love was. But now she was his, all right.

A dream coming true took as much out of a person as some terrible sorrow—how strange that was. She ached all over, and for a long time she couldn't sleep, and then it was early spring, the light was willow green, she was standing between Charlie's knees while he brushed her long golden hair. She had always known that she had long golden hair, and now everyone could see it.

But someone was crying; Charlie lifted her onto his lap.

"Hush now, darling. Hush now, Daddy's here." She stretched and relaxed, and tried to hold very still as he comforted her.

"Hush now, honey. I didn't mean to leave you, Alma. Seems like a man doesn't get a chance, these days. Honey, I won't ever leave you no more!"

She stirred and moaned, but Mammy didn't come. There was only Charlie, blue eyes awash with tears, holding her under the willow tree, and the light filtering through the long, yellow whips of new growth. He would never leave her. In her dream she turned and snuggled closer.

The instant Alma awoke she remembered everything. She was in such a state that she actually looked around for her father at the breakfast table, and then last night's weird dream came back, too. She kept her eyes on her cereal bowl, even after Uncle Ernie growled out the Tuesday blessing; he had one for every day of the week. She picked up her spoon, put it down again and then took it up, but she couldn't get down a bite of oatmeal. They might be able to see written on her face what she had done. But no one said a word about Howard. Naturally, Aunt Bernadine and Billy Jean wouldn't, in front of Uncle Ernie. Bobby, luckily, seemed to have forgotten all about his drowning and was thinking only of getting down to the barn to the new kittens.

Of course, Billy Jean brought it up the minute they

were alone, loading the dishwasher. "So what happened? I nearly died when I came back, and Mamma told me!"

"Oh, we just drove around. He was in one of my classes last year. We had this dotty old English teacher."

Billy Jean scowled and flooded the sink with hot water. "Lucky. Getting to go out with any boy you want, while I'm cooped up here like a baby."

"They're not exactly lining up for me, you know. Dee wouldn't let me go either, until after my birthday."

"It's medieval, the way he treats me. He wouldn't like it if he knew you went out last night, either. But don't worry, Mamma won't tell him. He figures there's only one thing could be going on. He'd be sure you were doing it with that boy the minute the car door was shut."

Alma wiped and rewiped the refrigerator door; she had a strange feeling that she would go on wiping until she had covered every gleaming inch of Aunt Bernadine's kitchen.

"Hey, hand me the sponge, Alma. That's enough. I suppose you're going out with him again."

"I don't know. He didn't ask me." If only she could tell someone; it was just too much to have all to herself. She looked wistfully at Billy Jean, now flinging hand lotion on her hands. But she couldn't possibly understand what Alma had done, just gone ahead without a murmur and done. The distance that had closed between them since she came out opened again. Who would understand? Wilma didn't have sex with boys, she realized at once; of course she didn't. Nor did Dilly . . . She couldn't tell them, either. It wasn't like it was in the movies, at Oaklon, she thought sadly. Or all those magazine articles—seventy percent of all high school students having regular sex, or whatever it was. Oh, it happened in Oaklon; unwillingly, she thought of Howard, and Myrna. But she would bet most girls here waited for their weddings—well, their engagements, probably. They had hope chests. Dilly had started embroidering pillowcases for hers years ago. Dilly and Wilma were both putting things away; nice girls with nice families, they'd have church weddings. She was Dee Jenkins Ryder's daughter, so she had sex. It was a sordid little thought that she squashed at once.

Maybe Howard wouldn't be back, and she would just have this amazing memory to cope with. No, he would call; tonight he would call and beg her to quit her job, to come out to Oakley and him for the rest of the summer. "Where's the aspirin, Billy Jean? I have the most god-awful headache."

"Your period? I always get a blinding one the day before. Oh Alma, I'm glad for you, I really am." Billy Jean turned and hugged her. "At least you can tell me how it is out there, in the normal world."

Alma laughed, but her mouth was dry. For the first time ever, she longed for her Oakley visit to be over. If Howard didn't call—but he must!—at least Dee would never know anything about it, and it could be her secret forever. But he had to call. It was masochistic to be so horribly sure he never, never would.

Thursday night Alma sat, suitcase between her knees, waiting for Dee and Roger. MicMac was opening tomorrow, cranking up for the long Fourth weekend. The Bradshaw boys down the road were already shooting off bottle rockets. It sounded like a real barrage, a whole town being wasted.

Aunt Bernadine, needlepoint on her lap, sat with her in the front room, where they could see through the bay window's lace curtains. "When are you coming back out, honey? It was just like old times having you here."

"I had a marvelous time," Alma said quickly. "It was really great." It was partially true, during the days, but each evening she had turned to stone, waiting for the call that didn't come.

Aunt Bernadine chuckled. "And that nice boy, taking you for a ride. A school friend of yours, saving Bobby—I can't get over that."

"We were just in the same class." She swallowed hard, and for her own sake said firmly, "He's got this other girl, I think."

"Downright handsome. You know who he reminded me of? Charlie. Oh yes, your father was a looker when he was young, before—" Aunt Bernadine bent closer to her needlepoint. "Well, never mind. But don't be too sure you won't see him, honey. You don't ever know what's going to be."

Alma saw the headlights of Roger's car. She buried herself in Aunt Bernadine's arms, wordlessly thanking her for everything, and especially for the hope she had just been given.

six

"PHONE ERNIE TO PICK YOU UP AFTER CHURCH tomorrow, baby."

Alma hadn't taken her bath yet. She sat in her Mic-Mac uniform, dull-eyed, watching Dee put on the finishing touches of a makeup job she had evidently started as soon as she finished her Saturday chores. Roger was taking her to a big dairyman's party in Sacramento; there was no time to drive Alma out to Oakley, Dee explained, pulling on the sheerest possible pair of pantyhose. The pants part was a black and red butterfly design, also sheer. They would be staying over with the people who were giving the party, she said, and then go to the Sunday dirt bike races.

"I hate to leave you here alone overnight, but I guess it'll be all right this once. You go out to Oakley in the morning with him. We'll pick you up Monday night. Honey, go take your bath; you won't feel so tired."

Alma wished she weren't just sitting here, watching her mother get so fixed up, in that lacy little half-slip and flowery bra. She knew what would happen later between her and Roger. She bit her lip. Dee would be surprised to know how much Alma understood now about her sex life. It was embarrassing to listen to her

67

stories about "staying over with friends." She shook her head and got up.

"I'm going to soak for hours. Have a good time, Dee." She ran the water for the long, relaxing bath she really needed. If only she could just say, "Oh, come off it. Any moron can see that you and Roger are lovers. So what? I don't care." And go on to explain she wasn't a virgin anymore, now she knew all about sex. She couldn't even begin to imagine Dee's reaction. She'd probably explode in a million pieces.

Laying in the steaming water she remembered that she still hadn't written to Charlie. She must do it tonight, because Aunt Bernadine would ask her first thing tomorrow. Hard as it was to fill a page, it was easier than face-to-face conversations with him, both of them desperately trying to find something to say. She didn't want, really, to ride out with Uncle Ernie after church, listening to him rave on about the gospel, but after getting through the last week, and then this one, she knew she simply couldn't go on without going back to Oakley. She wouldn't see Howard, of course, but she might see his car, parked out front at Petroni's, and she would know he was working in the orchards, not a half mile away. That would help her taper off, so to speak.

She hadn't meant to say a word about Howard to the girls unless he called her, but the pressure seemed to build independently inside her, and finally, Tuesday at work, as they cleaned up for the next shift, she had blurted it out.

"Hey, guess who I saw out at my cousin's when we were laid off. Howard Babcock. I really did."

Dilly finished the count of beef patties. "Fifty-two. Mike said Howard had a job this year. You know

68

Mike's folks won't let him work in the fruit? A big, strong guy like him?"

But Wilma, wiping the big range, had stopped to listen. "What was Howard doing at your cousins?"

"Well, it was really kind of exciting." But before she could tell them about Bobby drowning, Mr. Gladburn bustled back in and wasted time telling them to do exactly what they were doing. "Shipshape, troops!"

When he left, she had told the whole story, even the cake. "Then he asked me if I wanted to go for a ride."

"Sure he did," Dilly scoffed. "You wouldn't have kept news like that to yourself all this time!"

"Okay. If you don't want to believe it . . ."

"Alma! You are the wierdest. Come on, what happened?"

She had begun to wish she hadn't said a word.

"Oh, you know. We talked about Miss Murdoch, and he told me his mother's in Denver this summer, drying out somewhere I bet. And Myrna's going to that fancy art school in Mexico."

"Give, girl, give," Dilly urged. "Are you going to see him again?"

She had shaken her head, suddenly trembling. "I'm not going back out there to find out." And yet, as she said it so bravely, she realized she couldn't hold out much longer.

"He's got that car. He could come in to see you any evening, couldn't he?" Wilma asked gently.

She had shrugged and shaken her head as if it didn't matter that he hadn't come, hadn't called.

She ran more water in the tub, wishing now she'd said nothing about him. She was simply not herself yet. No wonder her imagination had started to go out of control, alarming her at night with all sorts of feverish ideas.

Dee pounded on the door. "There's some boy here to see you! Honey, Roger's here too, and we've got to go. I told that boy to wait for you out on the porch. Don't you let him in the house with me gone."

Alma's heart was banging so loudly she didn't hear the door slamming after Dee. She pulled on her new white jeans; in a dream she brushed her hair. She applied some of Dee's lip gloss, wiped it off, and at last went out, trying to open the screen door casually.

"Oh! It's you."

"This is such bad news? Okay, I'll leave quietly." Nelson wheezed out a laugh, but she could see he was taken aback by her reaction. His eyes behind the big glasses narrowed defensively.

She made herself laugh, and sat down on the steps. "No, no. I'm really glad you came over." After the sharp, deep thrust of disappointment, she was glad. It was so much better than being alone.

"Never would have guessed, by the look on your face. You expecting someone else?" But he sat down beside her, as if he knew just as well as she did that no one else was going to come.

"Don't be silly." Howard didn't even know where she lived in town, probably, and he couldn't care less.

Nelson rubbed his fat chin, "I didn't think you had a steady, but one never knows. Just slip me the word, and I'll clear out."

"Come on, Nelson. Do I have to beg you on my knees to stay? I'm free to see anyone I want. Howard Babcock, anyone . . ." She had this need just to say his name out loud.

"The steamy jock with the profile, right? Jimmy pointed him out. Don't tell me that's yours."

70

"I just said I went out with him, that's all."

"I know that type—just the dude all the chicks put out for."

"Why do you talk like that? Because with you it's all talk?"

"But not you, right? You're getting some action."

She turned away from him. "Why come around just to fight with me?"

"As a matter of fact, I didn't come around just to fight with you. After a mere seven weeks, the movie's changed. Yes siree. I thought we might take in this here new film."

It was a great idea, a godsend really, and later, when they walked home under the sycamore trees, she tried to tell him. "Thanks, Nelson. I was kind of down until you came along tonight." Of course Howard wouldn't call, thinking what he probably did about her, the original pushover, if he gave that evening a thought at all. She knew that, and yet she knew if she had the chance to do it over, she would do exactly the same. No matter how much it pained her. He did belong to her, in a secret sense, even if he never spoke to her again, if he went back to Myrna Logan tomorrow. He was hers in the same way that some mythical Daddy who didn't exist anymore, who had nothing to do with poor Charlie, was hers, in her head.

Nelson turned her around gently. "You're okay, you are. In a way it's better than coming on strong with the old beauty and image, you know? The way you start looking better all the time to someone, the more he looks? He'll be back, your classy jock." He spoke gently, too.

"He won't. But you're sweet, Nelson. You kind of grow on a person, too."

"The fungus people, that's us." He smiled, but most

of his big face was quiet, as if he knew she was still trapped in something else, in some adult action he couldn't follow.

"I can't ask you in, Nelson. My mother's gone, and she has these weird ideas."

"That's okay. See you soon." She watched as he lumbered down the street. It was too bad a boy as nice as Nelson had hips like that.

It was too late now to phone Aunt Bernadine, but that didn't matter. She'd be on the church steps in the morning and ride out with Uncle Ernie. For the first time all week she slept soundly—too soundly. When she awoke the sun was shining hotly—she lunged for the clock. Uncle Ernie had left church half an hour ago. She lay back and tried to plan some kind of a day. Wash her hair, go over to Dilly's. She must get right up and phone her or Wilma or someone, not lie there and think. She moved quickly, getting the Sunday paper in from the porch, scrambling her eggs. The expanse of sunshine gleaming on the empty kitchen table made her lonelier than ever. She piled more honey on her toast and resolutely turned to the funnies.

Someone was pounding on the front door.

She clutched the newspaper tightly. It was him; it had to be. She looked down at her nightgown and sprinted back to the bedroom for the new misty blue quilted robe Dee had given her for Christmas.

She opened the door and looked up into his face, still panting. "Hi."

Howard said nothing, and then he smiled. The beautifully modeled nose and mouth, those eyes; it was almost painful actually seeing him again.

Alma stepped back and spoke as easily as she could. "Come in. Have some toast? I'm alone; my mother's away for the weekend."

He still didn't say anything, looking around their living room. For a curious moment she had the feeling of it being foreign to her eyes as well, and suddenly too colorful, too crowded. She dropped slices of bread in the toaster, put the kettle on, trying to cover her emotion. "Coffee?"

"No thanks." She noticed then how sad he was. "We're not picking today," he said, as if that weren't evident. He looked down moodily; he was wearing expensive-looking riding boots. "I wanted to see if you were okay."

Alma choked and coughed on toast crumbs. "Why wouldn't I be okay?" She wondered why she was so quick to answer, defensively, like that.

"Thank God. Hey, I wanted to say I'm sorry for what happened that night. I didn't intend that—I got carried away."

She brushed her numb fingers on her robe front. "That's all right." But it wasn't all right at all. She had a feeling of having been hit, hard; she raised her face to him. Speaking through waves of despair, she asked, "You didn't like it? I mean, you didn't like me? I thought it was all right. Of course I don't know . . . how, or anything. But I thought it was great." She repressed sternly the growing upheaval inside. It occurred to her, as if from a long way away, that she was a terrible liar. It hadn't been great—it had been shocking and it hurt, but since it had been Howard that didn't matter.

"That isn't what I mean, Alma. You were so terribly, terribly sweet. But the thing is . . . I didn't have any right to do that. You shouldn't have let me—but I guess you didn't understand that."

"I still don't," she mumbled. "I just thought it was great. I know about you and Myrna and all, but I just thought it was great." Time was running out; he was going to turn and leave. She thought fast and decided to risk everything. "You know, I always had this crazy passion for you? Ever since first grade. Isn't that unbelievable? But I did, Howard, I always did. And wow, when you came around like that, well, I couldn't resist." She could feel his gloom lightening—this intrigued him; she breathed easier. "So it wasn't your fault at all, you see. It was me, wanting you so much. I guess I really should be thanking you." Yes, it was working. His glance met hers and locked. He smiled, that teasing, childlike smile, that caught her up in all of its sweetness.

"Secret passion, no kidding? Well, if you put it that way. You know, you have the shiniest, blackest eyes. Like a little mouse." He put his hand slowly on her shoulder, slipping it under the robe, under the thin nightgown, and running his palm along her warm shoulder. He held her close and then closer—she thought of Dee, suddenly, when Nelson had come by. *Don't you bring him in the house.* As she kissed Howard passionately back, she shivered and smiled inside, thinking how outraged her mother would be. But she wasn't there. The house was very empty of everything but the two of them. Slowly, wordlessly, she led him into the bedroom.

In the middle of the afternoon they went to Meely's for pizza. Howard chose a back booth and grinned at her across the murky table. "You're a real morale lifter. I figured this as a way, way down day. Now I just might make it through 'til sundown. You've really got the knack of taking a guy's mind off of his troubles."

"I'm sorry you have troubles." Gently she put her hand on his. Was it his mother? She wished she could get him to talk about her, and she'd tell him about Charlie. She looked at him, yearningly. It had, this time, really been making love. How fantastically different than in the orchard. She would never be free of him now. . . .

"Things have been worse. There have been rockier days." His hand tightened on hers. "You wouldn't know, a sweet little girl like you, but there was one whole summer when I couldn't seem to get out of bed. I mean I couldn't do it. I'd push at the old sheet, and then I'd start to sweat and shake, and I'd nearly pass out. You don't know what I'm talking about, do you?"

Alma shook her head slowly. "I used to feel just awful when I was little, and my parents would fight, I remember that." The tightness in her chest, as if she were suffocating in the hot hate between them. "I'd have to run away and hide. But not wanting to go on at all—no, I can't imagine that. What did you do, that summer?"

"Let's not go into it. It was the all-time low. I swallowed some sleeping pills and Myrna rushed me right to the emergency room—real prime-time drama. It all caved in on me that summer, but then we made up, and Mother got well. I wish they'd hurry that pepperoni —I'm starving."

Alma forgot her own concern. To think of Howard actually wanting to die!

"Hey you," he said softly. "Stop staring at me. It's okay. I survived. I'm alive, didn't you notice?"

But her thoughts went on, independently it seemed. He would leave her, and no matter how much that hurt, she knew she wouldn't want to die; she'd have all of these marvelous memories; that alone would be reason to go on.

"I shouldn't bore you with my life and times." He

looked into her eyes again. "I should leave you alone. I meant to. I came in to town today, full of the best of intentions, wanting to apologize for seducing you while my girl's away. And you saw what happened." He laughed ruefully.

Somehow it was understood that she didn't have the right to object to him talking about Myrna. Through the wave of humiliation his laughing words set off, it brushed through her mind to tell him what was bothering her, but she realized in time how silly it would have sounded. How unforgivable.

"She's a great girl, your Myrna." Alma couldn't tell if she was being sarcastic to punish him or herself. "She's got everything together." She did, too. Lead cheerleader, Senior Queen. "You're the swinging couple." She could feel the lumps of pizza in her stomach turning to acid.

"Some couple. She cuts out for the entire summer. But it was my fault. I was wearing her down with my moods. She was right to go."

"Howard." She couldn't bear another word. "Do you mind if we talk about something else? The weather? The price of peaches? There must be something." She marveled at the way she had said that. As if she were just bored, hearing about Myrna, instead of being torn in a hundred pieces.

Howard flushed, as if a little ashamed, and then grinned. "When you do speak up, you've got a sharp little tongue. But you're right. She has nothing to do with me and you."

He paid the check and they left, but not before Alma had noticed Dilly and Mike in the corner table. "Look who's over there."

Howard grabbed her arm and propelled her through the door. "Come on, come on."

Her cheeks flamed, but she didn't say anything until they were driving away. "Have to be careful who you're seen out with, Howard?"

He drove faster, not looking at her. "I don't give a damn who sees me doing what, or who writes what to Myrna. What blew up suddenly between us is private, isn't it? It's like something out of a dream, the way we just came together. It was very special and private, and I want to keep it that way."

Her heart melted, and she held his hand wordlessly all the way home. It didn't matter how forlorn their duplex looked when they pulled up in front, the tiny patch of lawn scuffed and brown. They kissed passionately, and he was silent. But before he left, he touched her face very gently, and whispered, "It was very special; you know it was."

Later, when she thought it over, she couldn't see the difference between keeping it private and keeping it quiet. Still, for him, too, it was something out of a dream; he had said so. He hadn't said it was his cherished dream coming true or anything like that, but it was fairly close. He hadn't made a date to see her again, either. *It was very special. Was.* He didn't mean anything by that. Maybe when she told him about Charlie, and he understood how much they had in common . . . If only Dee would come home. She was alone too much, that was the thing. If she had been lucky enough to have had parents who stayed together and were around more, maybe she wouldn't have wanted Howard so much, and they would have become friends first. But she knew that was a cop-out, blaming Charlie and Dee for what she'd done.

It was wrong just to have sex with him on the sly. Especially after today. Now she knew how powerful sex was, how it could really get you addicted. . . . That's what he was doing, just having sex. Would he have hustled her onto that blanket so fast if he hadn't sensed the rules didn't apply to people like her and Dee? No, it wasn't like that. He had been carried away with passion, but she had been carried away with love. She wouldn't be again, although now it was passion and love mixed together. They didn't really know each other. Howard didn't want to know her better; he was just marking time until Myrna got back, she thought as she changed the bed.

But she mustn't think in terms of time, just now.

It was so quiet she could hear the old refrigerator out in the kitchen clicking on and off. The faucet dripped in the sink.

That week passed without a word from him. She lived through it without breathing, it seemed. Business got better and better at MicMac's; she was paralyzed by the monotony of handing out Mickburgers, french fries—and vanilla, strawberry or chocolate shakes—by the slowed down evenings after work by the mute phone. When Dee was out, she covered the phone with a towel.

Saturday night she hung around, again watching Dee dress to go out. It would have been pointless to think of going to Oakley. Anyway, just as Dee and Roger were leaving, Nelson came up the walk. Dee ran back to the door.

"Now remember, you're not to entertain him in the house."

"That little chick your mum?" Nelson watched admiringly from the porch as Dee got into Roger's car, with a flash of legs and high heels. "Aha." He said it as if it explained something to him.

Then he turned to her. "Tonight—are you ready for

this—the drill is a visit to the artist's studio." He leered grotesquely, arching his eyebrows, one after the other. Alma couldn't help giggling. "You will come see my etchings, yes, *Liebchen,* yes?"

When they got to his house, he took her up the front steps. "The old studio's in the garage, but we've got to do a thing with the parents. Let's get it over with."

Nelson's mother, a round, fat little person who looked just like him, and his father, also round and fat, but looking more like a pleasant walrus with that big gray mustache, were watching television. They jumped up, faces aglow, when Nelson walked in with her.

"So this is the new friend. What a pretty name, Alma. Sit here by me." Nelson's father drew her down on the sofa, while his mother scuttled into the kitchen, calling anxiously, "Play some music, darling!" She seemed terrified that Alma would be too bored to stick around.

Nelson put on some records—classical ones, to her surprise. She could tell by the way he handled them, and the way he sat listening, that this was his kind of music. After awhile, his mother tottered out of the kitchen with cookies, Twinkies, candies, celery sticks and bottles of Diet Pepsi and ginger ale.

"What do you like to drink, Alma? Serve her more ice, Nelson. Surely you want more than one cookie."

Nelson loaded her plate, and then his own—especially with chocolates. His father cleared his throat and said sadly, "Mother made the celery sticks for you, son."

"Righto, Dad." Nelson put everything back

His mother said proudly, "He's on a diet. He's lost two pounds."

"In about two years." Nelson did his wheezy laugh and chomped celery.

"It's so nice for Nelson to have a new friend. He's been so lonely since we moved from the city." His mother leaned closer to Alma. "Always been such a quiet boy. He buries himself in his music and that photo lab."

Most people would have died to hear their mothers talk like that, but Nelson just winked at Alma. He seemed to know that his mother couldn't help herself, that she didn't know anything about the brash way he came on outside the house, a cover-up, of course. He *was* shy, like his mother said.

After a lot more questions and food—it was almost as if they were trying to fatten her up, to match Nelson—the two of them escaped.

"Sorry to put you through that," Nelson said, as soon as they got out to the garage. "Believe it or not, that made their evening. Their month, probably. Want a choc?" He had smuggled out half the box and explained, between gulps, "I'd diet if I could; it means so much to them. Who am I bulling? It'd mean a lot to me, too, to escape this lardo. But no can do."

"I bet you could. I mean not all at once, but listen, once I looked into that Al-teen stuff, you know, because of my father?" Last time, she'd told Nelson all about Charlie. He was a good listener. "You could do it the AA way. One hour at a time? Like right now you go until ten o'clock, say, without eating any chocolate."

"Jeez, I don't know." Nelson gave her a look. "So far all I can swing is going through the motions around them."

"If you can do that, you can do one hour a time away from them. You really love your parents, don't you?"

"Ah. They're harmless. Listen, it's no big turn-on for them, either, having a fat slob for their son. You're so lucky being just right the way you are. You don't know how it is when your own body is your worse enemy."

Alma smiled, a little grimly. "I think I have some idea."

"You? I don't get it."

She laughed; she could feel herself getting really silly. "Neither do I, Nelson, neither do I!" She pulled herself together. "Private joke. Forget it. You'd be so handsome if you were a little lighter," she said tactfully.

Nelson raised his eyebrows like Groucho Marx again. "*Then* you wouldn't be able to resist me, right? Now this is the immersion sink." He went on to show her all his development stuff and explained so well that for the first time Alma understood just how film is developed. The evening sped by.

But the next day, Sunday, she awoke as if on fire. She had to get out to Oakley for her days off. She left a note for Dee—who was not home yet—and met Uncle Ernie on the church steps. Doggedly, she endured his rehash of the day's sermon all the way out to the ranch.

Aunt Bernadine greeted her with hugs of delight, and Bobby dragged her off to see the kittens first thing. As they were coming back up the kitchen steps, the phone rang with a special, special sound. Of course it was him.

"My spies tell me you've just arrived."

Alma couldn't speak.

"I'll pick you up around eight tonight?" Howard went on, so lightly. She nodded violently, almost forgetting to speak aloud, not caring that she was grinning like an idiot in front of Aunt Bernadine and Billy Jean.

She put the phone down and danced Bobby madly around the room.

Howard turned the car radio up high, and they sailed along the highway. Now she could begin to believe she was there, actually beside him, and she felt herself glowing with happiness. How golden red the peaches were; it gave her a pang of pleasure to see them clustered under the dark green leaves. The branches of the trees swayed low with their heavy freight.

He parked in the same walnut orchard and reached for her hungrily. She responded helplessly, despite all of her good resolutions. She had planned to make him talk to her this time, to let them get to know one another, become friends. Then she wouldn't feel this awful loneliness, even when they did make love. Probably all she had to do was just mention what was on her mind, and he would reassure her. But Howard reached for her, and it was all happening again.

Afterward, he offered her a joint, but she shook her head. "I don't want any more new experiences just now." She watched as he went through a little ceremony of lighting up and sucking in the sweet smoke. They must get on friendlier terms. She began a conversation. "Where are you going to college, Howard? Stanford? You wouldn't have any trouble getting in, with your grades."

"Is that where you're planning to go?"

She blushed; he must have thought she was conniving to go where he did, as if they could ever afford Stanford. "I'm not going anywhere. My mother doesn't want me to."

"Crazy. And I'm going only because Mother's little heart is set on it."

"How is your mother?" Now he would tell her.

Howard frowned and rolled slightly away from her. "Throw me that shirt, will you? What have you heard about my mother?"

The truth had worked before. "I've heard that she drinks. And I'm sorry, Howard. I mean, if it's true."

"Oh, it's true. Let me put your mind at rest. That woman drinks, she has drunk, and she will keep on drinking, no matter what they try. She's in some drying out place in Denver now, if you really want to know. She's not visiting any friends. Hell, she doesn't have any friends. Too busy getting stinko to have friends instead of bridge partners. Now then, anything else I can clear up for you?" He glared at her, as if it were all her fault.

"Don't be mad. I only brought it up because I have the same problem. It's the same for me! My father! He's always going off on these drunks. He's getting over one right now; I thought you might have heard about him. In the hospital last spring, arrested for drunk driving, everything." Proudly she kept nothing back.

"No, I hadn't ever heard that." He inhaled the smoke. "For years I didn't let on that I knew. We played quite a game, me pretending she wasn't stoned out of her skull every afternoon when I got home from school, and her pretending she could focus on the A's on the report card, and sure, she'd come to the Cub Scout cookout, if she got over the flu in time. You know something, Alma? It was easier that way, a hell of a lot easier. The first time I let her know that I knew, that I was on to all the bottle caches, and the glasses of ice water that were vodka, I've never felt like such a no-good rat, before or after. The look on her face—it would have been more human if I'd hit her, smashed her one right between the eyes. And I thought I was clearing the air." He laughed bitterly. "As you might have guessed, that was the summer I almost checked out."

Alma reached for his hand and held it against her cheek. "My dad's always so sorry, afterwards. That's the worst part. The way he cries and keeps on begging everyone in sight to forgive him."

"Knowing the other kids knew, everyone in town knew. All my life I've had to carry that around. But this last year . . . she's dying, I think. Getting wispier and fading; the booze is getting her. And she's so beautiful—or was. My mother was a very beautiful woman."

"My dad—" But then she had enough sense to give up talking about her problem and just held his hand. They didn't make love anymore that night, but when he brought her home, they sat awhile in each other's arms, as if he were unwilling to let her go, as if there was some kind of solace between them. She couldn't talk to him, not tonight. His thoughts were miles away, probably with his mother.

At the door, he kissed her gently. "We're really going full blast with the picking now. No more days off, my dear relative says." He could have been saying he wouldn't be coming to see her anymore.

Alma was too discouraged to even wash her face when she got inside. Telling him about Charlie hadn't brought them any closer really; Howard wasn't interested in her problem parent, only his. What would be the point of seeing him anymore—if he did call? In a few weeks Myrna would be back and their secret world, such as it was, would have to come to an end. It was a very limited world. She closed her eyes and saw him before her: that perfect face, shaped the only way a face should ever be. She would have to hang on as long as she could, dangerous as it was. She fumbled for the aspirin she had started taking each night to dull her thoughts enough so she could get to sleep.

"Honey, you're not eating a thing. Look at that. You'll waste away to nothing." The family had already had breakfast when Alma came down, but Aunt Bernadine had happily stirred up fresh pancakes for her. "It's that boy. Lovesick, you are." She rubbed Alma's head lovingly. "Oh, I can just imagine."

Thank God Aunt Bernadine couldn't imagine. "Summer's a very bad time, isn't it! Oh, I wish it were over. No, I wish my father were here." Alma was as surprised as Bernadine at that outburst, but often now at night she awoke to his fading figure and understood that he had been in her dreams again, but that was the Daddy of her childhood. What did Charlie have to do with any of it?

Aunt Bernadine was pleased at such daughterly feelings. "He'll be back, one of these days, good as new. Poor child." She smoothed Alma's hair again. "Just wearing your heart out over that boy."

Billy Jean, reading the newspaper in the window seat, looked up and snorted. "I wish I had your troubles, Alma. Man, I'll trade, any day." She had no idea at all what she was saying.

There was some release in getting up to clear away the dirty dishes. Later—oh, what could she do later? She no longer dared to be alone in her fig tree, reading. Reading was no longer possible anywhere. The thoughts of Howard that pulled at her so would surge in, and the fear that was beginning to insist on being recognized would return.

"Aunt Bernadine! Let me do the cleanup."

But Aunt Bernadine had gone to wheel Aunt Selma out in the sun and tend to her chickens. Billy Jean was still hunched over the paper. Alma carried out dishes and looked quickly around for something else to do, hoping Bobby or Rhonda or someone would come along to talk to her. She scraped her untouched pancakes into the garbage and loaded the dishwasher. She wouldn't see him again. Far better that way. From now on she would stay in town on her days off. It couldn't be true. She scrubbed the sink again and got out the floor mop and brushes.

Later, Rhonda came by, a kitten rolled in her skirt.

"Come down to the barn, Alma, and play with me and Bobby. We're hiding the kittens from Old Blue." Old Blue was the perennial mother cat, the best mouser in the San Joaquin Valley, and highly valued by Uncle Ernie and Ben.

Aunt Bernadine came back up the porch steps, banging the screen door. "It's going to be a real scorcher today. I'll have to watch Auntie doesn't get too warm. I fixed her under the Bougainvillaea for now. Why, Alma! And the floor, too. Aren't you ashamed, Billy Jean, setting in there while she does all this work alone!"

"Don't scold her, Aunt Bernadine, I liked having something to do." She tried to make light of her restlessness. "I'm just blasting off with energy today. Come on, Rhonda, let's go."

"You're a good girl, Alma, always said you were my good girl."

Pretending she didn't hear, Alma clattered after Rhonda down the steps. Today it was going to be especially bad. She must keep moving.

They climbed up to the loft where Bobby sat in the hay, Old Blue's kittens clamped like leeches on his fat arms and legs. "She found them all, Rhonda. This one's my best one, see, Alma. It's just like Old Blue."

She picked up the bluish striped kitten and felt the fragile neck joints under the silky fur. The kitten looked up at her out of round, clean eyes and the cold lump inside her melted a little. How sweet they were.

Bobby tried to cradle all the kittens at once on his lap, but they crawled out as fast as he picked them up. After a while, Rhonda went back to the house to get milk for them. The sun came in slanted rays through the hay window. A hen cackled from across the corral; sadness like peace flooded through Alma.

"You remember me, Bobby, if I don't come back to Oakley anymore." She hugged him fiercely.

"Let me go. Alma, why won't you come back, why?" Bobby's face started to crumple; he clutched at her shirt.

"I didn't mean that. Well, someday, maybe, I couldn't come, for a while. Someday." But her voice broke a little.

Bobby pulled at her. "No! You come, Alma. You come all the time!"

She had to quiet him down, or he might say something to Rhonda. "Sure, I'll come. I was just talking. I'll come."

He turned happily back to the kittens. A wave of sickness swept over her; she sat very still until it passed and then wiped the cold sweat from her face.

Rhonda appeared at the ladder top with a plastic pitcher of milk, and soon the kittens' flowery heads were clustered around their bowl.

"My goodness, isn't it warm." Through the loft door they could see and hear Aunt Bernadine and a reluctant Billy Jean picking peas in the garden. "Where have all the children got to? Billy Jean, honey, you run push Auntie around more in the shade, will you?" The heat shimmered, making silvery shadows below the rows of the tall, blond sweet corn.

"We're having snow pudding for dinner, Mamma says," Rhonda murmured, shaking back her blond, wispy hair.

"See, the chickens are taking their baths now." Bobby pointed to the old Leghorn hens scratching holes in the soft dirt by the tool shed and then fluffing the dust on their feathers. "I bet that's nice and cool."

"Why don't you go try it?"

He looked up to see if Rhonda were teasing. "That would be fun, wouldn't it, Alma?"

She must have answered. She remembered way back in June, that night Charlie went on his drunk, when she had thought she had said good-bye to Oakley. Good-bye seemed to be something you had to say over and over again. Of course she would see Howard again. To say good-bye, if nothing else . . . She tried to imagine how she would tell him, if the fear didn't fade away, but the scene simply refused to focus in her mind. Too wild. That proved it was only her imagination. The children squatted on the floor behind the kittens, trying to coax them to drink again. Her hands hidden in her lap, she counted again; for the hundredth time it came out the same way. It was over six weeks since her last period.

seven

IT WAS WORSE WHEN SHE DID MANAGE TO FORget for a little while, because when it flooded back in, it was almost more than she could bear. Like this morning at work. Mr. Gladburn, who drove them crazy anyway, with his constant pick-picky, had been needling Dilly about her Mickburgers.

"Look at the template, soldier. The template. How many times have I told you! Start with the relishes, left to right—" He snatched off his glasses and put them down, not quite on the edge between the range and the counter. "Cheese, patty, bun, bag—that's the drill." The girls watched, fascinated, as the plastic rims of the glasses slowly began to soften and add an acrid overlay to the greasy burger smell of their cramped quarters.

"You've got to keep your mind on what you're doing, soldier," he advised Dilly sternly, and the girls collapsed in fits of giggles.

Poor Mr. Gladburn looked around and had the grace to blush as he snatched up the now slightly warped glasses, and then clapped them back on. The girls went off in another fit, tears rolling down their cheeks.

"All right, all right. Show's over." He retreated to the supply room, and Alma went back to the counter, smothering her giggles—and then it hit her with such a force that she instinctively stepped back from the waiting customer. She took the order numbly, engulfed again.

It could be nothing more than nerves. She certainly had had a trying time these last few weeks; all that tension and uncertainty would throw anyone's period off. And the waves of nausea that were apt to strike, especially in the morning—anyone half out of her mind with worry would get those. Almost three weeks late now, but actually that wasn't so much. She had decided to assume she had just skipped a month, and to put it out of her mind until her period came around again; next week, Thursday, it was due. Then if it didn't come—oh, what then? "One MicMac, one large french fries, choc shake. That it?" She smiled desperately, idiotically, at her customer, a small, surprised kid in a faded Little League uniform.

She knew about birth control pills, of course—the lavender discs filled with tiny pills that Dee kept hidden in her pantyhose drawer—so why hadn't she protected herself? Or had she thought since it wasn't planned, adult sex, like Dee's, she wouldn't need anything? "You're just a baby." Dee was always saying that. But she had never expected to make love, any of the times. Or had she? Howard must have known, why hadn't he done something, worn something? she almost bumped into Dilly at the range, stunned by the sudden understanding. She had thought nothing so everyday as getting pregnant could happen, because he was so special.

"Alma, where are you! I've said twice that I've got a message for you, from Jimmy. Aren't you interested?"

She and Wilma got lunch break together and were

at the picnic table on the cinders out back. Alma turned her MicMac over and over in her hands, unable to take a bite. "Sure. What's the big news?"

"Well, if you aren't in too tight with the great Howard, or busy with Nelson, there's another sharp guy who's eying you. He asked Jimmy to see what he could do. Don't you want to know who?" Wilma's forehead and cheeks were flushed a lovely peach color from the heat.

"Not if you don't want to tell me. No, of course I want to know. Who is this guy with the great taste?" It was amazing how one could operate on two levels like this. Keeping the face on smile, even chewing food, everything normal and everyday, while just a little deeper in, one was drowning, drowning . . . in over the head and going down fast. Alma deliberately made her smile wider.

"Bradley Toner, that's who. He saw you at the movies the other night—with the great Howard, I suppose—and decided he'd never really taken a good look before. That's what he told Jimmy." Wilma, sweet Wilma, was so happy to bring her this news.

"It was Nelson who took me to the movies." Howard had never really taken her anywhere, except deep into the orchard at night—she had to close her eyes for a minute.

"Man, you're really branching out," Wilma said happily. "Nelson, and then Howard. You've come a long way, baby."

"You should only know." She smiled, but some of the hurt inside must have shown; she could tell by the sudden concern on Wilma's face, and she longed to blurt out her misery. But it might yet be all right; she must hang on until next week. "You tell Jimmy to tell

Brad he'll just have to wait his turn." She yawned, as if bored by the thought.

"Far be it from me to tell you, with all your men, what to do." Wilma gathered up her lunch scraps. "But what happens when Myrna comes back from Mexico?"

"A very good question." Alma shoved her uneaten MicMac back in the bag. "Yes, I would say that's a very relevant question."

Wilma said comfortingly as they went back in, "She's not here now, that's the important thing. Time's on your side."

Alma rushed to the rest room, just before she got sick, wishing Wilma hadn't said that about time.

Dee made an effort to seem pleased when Alma told her she wouldn't go out to Oakley Sunday and Monday.

"That'll be nice, baby." She added, "Roger wanted to take me up to Jackson Sunday, but I'll just tell him to forget it. I don't want to leave you here alone again. Say, what about that boyfriend out there?"

She had told Dee very little about Howard. How could she? Dee could accept her having a boyfriend—she'd loosened up that much—but she wasn't ready to accept the fact that her baby could have a love affair. It wasn't a love affair, anyway. It never had been.

"I'm not going to see him anymore. For a while." She had to add that, somehow. "I'm really bushed this week; I may be getting the flu. I'll just stay here and rest. So don't change your plans. I don't want you to disappoint Roger."

"Are you sure?" Dee seemed doubtful but relieved. "He was counting on it so much; thinks I put him second, anyway."

"He does?" Alma was surprised enough to forget her troubles.

"Well I do, of course; you always come first. But Roger, now there's a man with his own ideas." Dee laughed, but not cheerfully, and went on with her bill paying.

But Alma sat thinking. Was Dee serious about Roger? "Are you really interested in him? Like marrying him?"

Dee was silent, and answered finally, as if it weren't easy to say at all. "I'm interested all right, but he's not. Marriage again he doesn't need, he tells me."

She seemed on the verge of honestly confiding in Alma, for once. Could it be that she had a similar feeling about Roger—funny, bashful old Roger—that Alma had about Howard? It didn't seem possible, but she looked at her mother with new interest. If only they could talk to each other about this, the way they could about clothes and things that didn't really matter. If only she could tell Dee that she understood, that she knew how it was to want someone who didn't want you back the same way. But what would Dee say if she knew how experienced Alma was now? What would she say if Alma had to tell her she was pregnant?

The phone rang—for her—and it was, of course, Nelson. He wanted to take her to the new space movie opening Saturday night.

Dee was pleased. "He seems like a nice boy. If any of them are." She grinned almost shyly at Alma, as if she, too, wanted to be able to talk.

Alma didn't know how to answer that crack, though. But she said, quietly, "When Nelson brings me home Saturday, I'd like to ask him in, just to talk and have a snack. We're friends, you know. I mean, I realize you won't be here, but I'd like to do that."

Dee seemed surprised by this request, and maybe impressed by Alma's manner. "Well. I guess there's nothing to worry about. It's kind of silly not to let him in off the porch."

"It is silly. Thanks." How easy it was to get things you really didn't care that much about. It was far too late to worry about her being seduced anyway, if only Dee knew. She got up and fled to the bathroom and checked again. It was enough to keep her period from ever coming, the way she was compelled to check every fifteen minuts. She leaned her head against the cool porcelain of the sink and waited, dully, for the disappointment to ebb enough so she could go back out to Dee.

After the movie Saturday night, she invited Nelson in, thinking to herself about the energy people wasted over the wrong things, if they only knew it. Maybe she, too, was worrying about something needlessly. She opened the fresh pack of Fig Newtons.

"Not for me, I hope." Nelson grinned, a little shyly. "I haven't had any junk all week, and guess what? Another two pounds have bit the dust. My mother and father are half out of their minds with joy."

" 'Atta boy, Nelson. I knew you could do it." Alma shook his hand. "That's fantastic!"

"One hour at a time, the alkies and me. It works, but is it tedious. A real hardcore drag."

Alma congratulated him again, as she made them red zinger tea, not trusting herself to tell him she knew all about that one hour at a time routine. Getting through this evening, but not daring to look ahead to tomorrow, if it doesn't come. Oh, God, let it come this week. It was a relief, really, when Nelson went home and she could stop being cheerful and pretending she was her old self. With effort, she imagined that old self she had become so separated from. Dumb. Green. Living in a stupid dream. But so safe, so secure. Her period was due again by Thursday, and if it didn't come this time she would have to do something. She should be making plans right now, to help her get through these next days, until it came. She sat hunched in the wing chair, clutching her bare feet, glowing from the long hot bath she had run after Nelson left. These last weeks she had spent all of her free time in a hot tub. It hadn't helped, of course. She would have to tell Dee. No, she would make an appointment with Dr. Pershing on her own. She could never bring herself to do that, either. But to tell Dee . . .

She would have to. How much longer could she wait? Two months—a baby was pretty much formed in that length of time. A baby of her own. She should be drinking milk and all that, if it were really so. It couldn't, couldn't be so.

She wouldn't tell Dee, she would tell Howard. After all, it was his responsibility, just as much as hers. He should have known what was going on. But at the same time she had to admit to herself that he probably assumed that she was on the pill or something. And he had asked her if she was all right, that time he had come to the house. He hadn't been asking about her mental state, although she had chosen to think so at the time. Later, yawning, blessedly sleepy for once, she crawled into bed and found that she had decided something. If it didn't come Thursday, Howard would be the one to tell. It was his problem, too. But maybe, oh maybe, she had just skipped last month, and her period would be here on schedule. She went to sleep with her arms clenched defensively across her chest.

Friday evening she called Billy Jean. Thursday had been a bad day, a very bad day: an attack of nausea at breakfast that couldn't have been concealed from Dee if she herself hadn't been sick with cramps and still in bed. All day the conviction had grown that her period wasn't coming, ever again. She could tell Billy Jean had noticed the misery in her voice when she asked baldly if Howard had been around the weekend before.

"He didn't call either. I asked Mamma every day to make sure." There was a sad pause. "I'm sorry, Alma. Listen, they've been picking about sixteen hours a day over there, they really have. You come out Sunday, and if the peaches have peaked by then, I'll bet he'll be around."

Alma couldn't say a thing.

"You still there? Listen, he'll be around."

She hung up in a rush of tears, without even saying good-bye, and that night she had the drowning dream. It was she, not Bobby, who was at the bottom of the ditch. Every time she started to struggle upward to the surface of the water, she could see, so pale and green, all light glimmering above her, the fresh air, the outside world—just inches away—but some black force tugged her back down in again. She screamed and fought, her breath was going—she awoke with her heart jabbing a hole in her side, and found she was covered with sweat.

Dee stood over her bed, sleepily pulling at her shoulder. "Baby, what's going on? You had a regular nightmare going there! All right now? Why, you haven't had a nightmare since you was a toddler." And Alma remembered those long-ago nights when she would awake, finding herself in the kitchen, or once, a really scary time, she was out on the sidewalk in front of the project where they all lived. It was Charlie who found her out there, and his big warm hand led her back to the house. He heated milk for her and held her on his lap until she fell peacefully asleep again. The rest of the night she lay huddled under her sheet, staring at the ceiling. There was no way she could force herself to go out to Oakley, not this weekend.

She got through work the next day somehow, explaining her low spirits by saying she was getting the flu. She told Dee, and later Nelson when he phoned, the same story. She spent Sunday in bed reading old magazines and watching television, one program after another.

But Dilly had Mondays off too, and insisted on coming over that afternoon. "You would have given me the flu Saturday at work if I'm going to get it. I really need to talk to you."

Alma put down the phone. She would tell her, her oldest friend. What a relief it would be to share it with someone; Dilly might think of something she hadn't thought of herself; she also might have some news of Howard, through Mike.

It was Mike Dilly wanted to talk about. She burst into tears as soon as she got in the house, and poured out the whole story. They had had a fight Saturday night, and he still hadn't called. "I can't stand it any longer. Waiting and waiting, what if he doesn't ever call? What if that's it? Oh Alma, I think I'll just die— I can't go on without Mike!" She bit her lip. "I mean, I know you're kind of down because of Howard, but Alma, you never were his girl, really. I mean, you haven't seen him very much, and there's Myrna. But Mike and I have been together for months. You just don't know."

Dilly looked so woebegone she couldn't say anything about her own troubles. "Come on. I'll make you some red zinger tea. I'm into making tea for people lately. Nelson . . . hey, do you know he's really gone on a diet. Isn't that great?"

"Yeah. I'm so glad he's your friend, too. Old Howard didn't leave you high and dry anyway."

Alma gripped the teapot tightly. It was the perfect opening, but Dilly went on. "Wilma told be about Bradley Toner, too. If I were you, I'd call him right now. I wouldn't waste another minute moping around."

Alma poured out the tea. "Look who's talking. Call Bradley yourself." They both laughed and felt better, drinking the hot red tea. Later, she was glad she hadn't told Dilly. Howard was the one to tell first. She would go out there next week—she could do it—and give him the news.

Rhonda and Bobby were waiting out by the road when Dee and Roger dropped her off Saturday afternoon after her shift. Seeing them standing there, so solemn and expectant, the heaviness inside softened. The children grappled with one another over her suitcase, Rhonda, being stronger, winning the right to carry it. Bobby whimpered and Alma picked him up. The heft of his solid little body against hers was like a balm.

"I missed you so, honey. Have you been a good boy? How's Old Blue and the kittens?" Bobby wagged his bare feet and reluctantly she put him back down.

"I got a pencil box and a lunch box with Footley Fleas on it." He was starting kindergarten this year.

"I've got a new lunch box, too. Mine's just as new as yours, smartie." In three weeks school would start. How could time pass so quickly, so relentlessly? Where would she, Alma, be when high school started—she couldn't imagine. She followed the children into the house and allowed herself to be hugged and kissed by Aunt Bernadine.

"Billy Jean's down at the Bradshaws—she'll be so glad you got here this time. Come in and say hello to Auntie."

Auntie sat in her chair in front of the television, mouthing words to herself. Alma bent and kissed the network of wrinkles that was Auntie's dark cheek. "Hi, Aunt Selma. How're you?"

The old lady pulled away, muttering, "Don't fool me. I saw you putting those pills in my coffee."

Alma shrank back aghast, but Bernadine patted her arm reassuringly. "Don't mind what she says, honey. It's those serials she watches; just gets them all mixed up in her mind." Lovingly, Aunt Bernadine turned up the sound of the set. "There now, Auntie, go ahead and watch your program. We'll be in the kitchen."

She cut Alma a raisin-studded wedge of coffee cake, fresh from the oven. For the first time all week, Alma felt hungry. "This is marvelous. It looks like you're getting ready for a bake sale." The kitchen counters were covered with loaves of bread, squares of cinnamon rolls, and a big sheet cake.

Aunt Bernadine laughed. "I just have a feeling the Hinkels might come in tomorrow. They said they'd be down in August, and here it is half gone already, and we haven't seen hide nor hair of them."

"Why can't they phone you, or write, and tell you when they're coming? It seems to me the least they could do."

Of course Aunt Bernadine didn't see it that way. "They're so busy, up there in the city."

Alma wasn't really listening. She had brought her

new blouse to wear tonight when he came. He had to come. If he didn't phone, she would phone him.

When Billy Jean came in, she said admiringly, "That's a foxy shirt, Alma," and in a lower voice when her mother was in setting the table, "They stopped picking early this afternoon. On the way back from Bradshaw's, I saw the crew coming in."

While they were at supper a car turned down the driveway, and Alma jumped in her chair. But it was Mr. Petroni to tell Uncle Ernie it would be his turn to irrigate the next day. After they had washed up, Alma wandered restlessly in and out of the house, going with Rhonda to look for frogs in the little ditches around the alfalfa field. They had a clear view of the roads for miles around out there. Then she went with Bobby up to the dark-filled hayloft to check on the kittens. They scampered out the door, and Little Blue got stuck on the roof ridge. Ben brought the ladder and lifted her down, while Bobby shrieked.

It was ten after eight. Last time he had come at eight. "Bed time," she called desperately. "Come on, honey, want a piggy ride to the house?" She carried Bobby in and dumped him in the tub, not caring how the new shirt got splashed. It was eight-thirty-five by the time he was settled. Billy Jean was going to the second show with the Bradshaw girls and begged Alma to come along. "Be out when he calls. Serve him right."

She could only shake her head. "No, I'd really rather stay here and watch television." She went purposefully in and sat down with Auntie and Rhonda, but it was painfully hard to stay in her chair. Eight-forty; he wasn't coming. She would have to telephone him, then. She went out in the kitchen, where Aunt Bernadine was making pies. "Where's the telephone book?"

Aunt Bernadine indicated with her elbow the drawer

that held it. "I don't know, honey." Her floury hands paused in rolling out the dough. "You're sure it's the thing to do, to call that boy?"

"Yes. He told me to, if he didn't call me first." She knew it sounded fishy. With cold hands she took the directory over to the window seat and sat swinging her feet tightly in front of her while the number rang and rang. Someone had to be home over there, all that family, and the extra men there picking. She looked up the number again, to make sure it was right, and redialed. She stopped midway, the receiver pressed to her ear. A car was coming along Oakdale Avenue; it was turning in. She slammed down the phone and rushed to the bathroom, checking her hair, running water over her hands again, holding her breath until Aunt Bernadine called.

"Alma? Where are you, honey? Come see who's here!" There was a babble of voices. Not daring to think, she darted out to the kitchen, almost tripping on the suitcase in front of the stove.

"Dad!" She flung herself into his arms to hide the disappointment she knew must be on her face. "Hey, when did you decide to come back?"

Aunt Bernadine stood beaming at them, dusting the flour off her hands with her apron.

"Well, Alma! I was just hoping you'd be out here. How are you, darlin'?" Charlie's clear blue eyes were fixed on her alone, but he stopped grinning. "Why, you look thin." He turned to Bernadine. "Looks like she's been working too hard."

Aunt Bernadine made him sit down at the table and cut him a piece of coffee cake. "You must be hungry after that long bus ride and a taxi from town! You should have phoned. Now Alma's just fine. Girls like to be thin. Billy Jean's been starving herself all week—

nothing but grapefruit, that child." She gave Alma a glance that was easy to read: she wouldn't tell Charlie about Howard, not if Alma didn't want her to. "Your job will soon be over anyway, won't it, Alma?"

"School starts in three weeks." She made herself smile brightly for him. "How come you're back so soon?"

He took another bite of cake. "Your Uncle Leonard can't bake cake like this; now that's one good reason, right there. We finished his roof, and I got restless. Figured it was time to come back and see how all of you were getting along." He spoke with confidence. They could see perfectly well that he hadn't been drinking. He was brown and hearty.

"You're looking so well, Charlie!" Aunt Bernadine couldn't take her eyes from him. "Ernie's gone to his meeting at the parsonage, but he should be back before long. I better take you in to say hello to Auntie or she'll give me a real going over." They all trooped into the living room.

Auntie knew Charile all right. She gave a little cry of delight; there was even some color creeping into those dark old cheeks. "What did you bring me?"

He hadn't forgotten her. Carefully, he unlocked his suitcase and brought out a brightly studded pin which he fumbled around with until he had it fastened on Auntie's shawl. "Genuine turquoise, they told me at the Indian place." He'd brought one for Aunt Bernadine, and for Alma and Billy Jean there were bracelets, turquoise and silver. Of course he'd spent every cent Uncle Leonard had given him. He brought out a ring for Rhonda and fringed leather pouches for Bobby and Ernie.

"Just like Christmas!" Aunt Bernadine crowed. "You

always bring the best presents, Charlie." He blushed happily.

The bracelet was really neat. Charlie, one carryover from the golden Daddy days, was great on presents, when he had any money. Under cover of all the talking, Alma went over to the window and glanced sadly at the dark, empty road. Howard wasn't coming. She would have to deal with it on her own. When she came down to it, there was only one person she could tell. Aunt Bernadine. She could tell her anything; there would be no recriminations from her. But the thought of the sorrow her trouble would bring to that kind face . . .

Now Aunt Bernadine was busy with sheets and blankets for Charlie's bed. No, she wouldn't think of getting mad, but it would break her big heart in two. And she would have the burden of keeping it, a real sin in his eyes, from Uncle Ernie. But Aunt Bernadine would know what she should do next.

And action must be taken. More than eight weeks had gone by since her last period. She kissed Charlie good night, praying now of all times he would stay sober. She worked out her strategy: she would come down early, find Aunt Bernadine alone and tell her while they got breakfast. Yes, she was the one to tell; she wouldn't explode the way Dee, who had her own problems anyway, would. . . . Best to leave her out of it and tell Aunt Bernadine, who always had time for everyone.

eight

WHEN ALMA CAME DOWN THE NEXT MORNing, Aunt Bernadine was stirring up pancakes in her biggest bowl. Rows of bacon, the stripes of fat transparent already, were laid out on the grill. "I thought you'd sleep late when you got the chance, a working girl like you."

"I'm not tired." Alma got the plates down from the cupboard and began to deal them around the dining table. There wasn't a sound outside, except for the rooster, standing on the pasture fence, calling out at what seemed timed intervals. Like an echo, the Bradshaw's rooster down the road crowed in the pauses in between.

She must begin. "There's something I wanted to talk over with you." This was going to be hard, hard.

"What is it, honey? You didn't phone him after all, did you, that boy? I expect it's just as well."

Alma took a deep, unwilling breath. "Aunt Bernadine—"

"Shhh." They listened. Like a fretful kitten, Auntie was muttering and calling weakly from her room off the living room. "I bet she's in a mess." Aunt Bernadine wiped her hands and lumbered off.

Relieved, Alma went on with the table, and when her aunt still didn't come back, started on the pancakes.

"There you are, Auntie, all set." Aunt Bernadine parked Aunt Selma's wheelchair inside the door and took the dirty sheets on out to the washer on the back porch. "You get first crack at the pancakes this morning, looks like."

"Good morning, Auntie," Alma said, but Auntie twisted her lips and jerked her head.

Aunt Bernadine seemed amused. "I think she has you mixed up with that nurse on her program, the one that's been poisoning all the patients in General Hospital? I'll turn those, honey."

It would have been possible to talk in front of Auntie—she didn't understand a thing anymore—but Alma just couldn't bring herself to do it. Silently, she filled a plate with pancakes and rolled the old woman in her wheelchair up to the table in the other room.

Aunt Bernadine came in and bent over the plate. "There you are, Auntie." But the old woman whimpered to herself and then spat, deliberately. "My land, you're in a mood this morning. Spitting all over Alma's nice table. Now that was downright mean, honey." She wheeled her out into the living room and turned on her church program before coming back. "She's fixing to be a trial today, I can see that."

"I don't see how you stand it. All these years, and she's getting worse." Alma took off the plates to be washed again, and scrubbed at the plastic tablecloth. "She's really getting to be something else."

"But this here's probably her last summer. I don't think she'll make it through another winter. Ernie was checking on the cemetery lots just the other day. We better see to it now, he said, not leave it for bad weather."

"Do you think she knows, Aunt Bernadine, that she's going to die?"

"She knows, but part of her doesn't admit she knows. Makes her act up that way, knowing, but not wanting to know."

"I see what you mean, all right." Alma's heart cramped up again. But it was too late to tell Aunt Bernadine now, she could hear Uncle Ernie tramping down the hall. "I don't think many people would be so nice about taking care of her, like you always are." Auntie wasn't even Bernadine's own relative, but she didn't say that.

"Well, that's the way it goes, honey. We're all going to get old and die, same as we all got born." Cheerfully, Aunt Bernadine cracked eggs on the rim of the skillet.

Alma shivered, a wave of sickness was beginning. She nodded to Uncle Ernie as she darted out to the bathroom. Afterward, she washed out her mouth, sponged her face and hands, wiped the dampness from her hair and leaned out the bathroom window to sniff the roses all over the wall outside. Whatever was going to happen to her, and her baby, at least death and old age had nothing to do with it, and she felt comforted.

Charlie, his hair still wet from the comb, was at the table having his pancakes when she came back. He pulled out a chair for her next to him. "Sit down and eat. I don't like seeing you so skinny." At the other side of the big table, Uncle Ernie was hidden behind the Sunday papers.

"Give her that egg you just fried for me, Bernadine," Charlie urged. "Here now, put on lots of butter." With others around, Charlie had no trouble talking to her.

Luckily, now that the morning's sickness was out of the way, she could eat. Charlie kept looking at her.

"Never did see the sense of your taking a job this summer. But there never was no use arguing with you. Stubborn! But there, darlin', I don't want to scold you." Her being thin really gave him a topic.

"Now Charlie, she's just fine. And the money she's made this summer, all by herself. They've got to grow up, you know."

They kept on and on, and to shut it out, Alma ate steadily. "There's no harm in asking," Charlie was saying when she tuned in again. "With grapes coming on, the cannery's bound to be running eight or ten weeks longer."

"You're going to get your job back at Pacific Peaches, Dad? That's great." He looked so well now that he was off the drink she wouldn't be surprised if they did take him back. "You call me up Tuesday night now, and tell me if you got on." Bernadine and Charlie both smiled with pleasure at this daughterly concern. His job was something they could talk about. When he saw her swelling up with pregnancy that would give them something else to talk about. . . . She got up to clear the table, shaken by her crazy thoughts.

Bobby and Rhonda appeared for the next round of pancakes. Charlie followed Ernie outside, insisting he could do the irrigating all himself, and Ernie could go in to church. But as much as Uncle Ernie hated getting the water on Sunday morning, he wouldn't let anyone else, not even Ben, oversee his irrigating.

Billy Jean was the last down. She knew she didn't need to ask if Howard had called. While the girls loaded the dishes, Aunt Bernadine worked on a mammoth potato salad. "I always think it's so pretty, nice rim of deviled eggs to finish off." Her square brown hands flew from slicing board to bowl. "Don't forget, Billy Jean. You promised your father to drive Rhonda in to Sunday School. You go get her ready now, honey."

Alma speeded up her stove polishing. Bobby had gone off with the men; this was going to be her chance. She must come straight to the point. *Guess what, Aunt Bernadine, I think I'm pregnant, Aunt Bernadine. How about that, Aunt Bernadine.* Dizzily, she wiped her hands on the dish towel and waited until Rhonda and Billy Jean tramped out, bickering about which one was making them late.

"Aunt Bernadine, I wanted . . . I've got something to tell you."

"Now's a good time, looks like, honey."

She took another deep breath and carefully wiped her hands again. "That boy, Howard Babcock."

Aunt Bernadine added a drop more Worcestershire sauce to her mix. "He'll call, honey, I just feel he will."

"That's not what I mean."

Aunt Bernadine straightened up. "Alma. A car's driving in right now."

They both hurried to the door. "Now didn't I tell you!"

The Hinkels' big Buick, the windshield spattered with crushed insects, drew up under the fig tree, and before they had the car doors open, they could be heard calling and laughing.

Aunt Bernadine, face alight, hurried down the porch steps. "Well, well, look who's here! And about time, too!" She exchanged pecks with Esther, but Bill swooped her in for a real kiss. The children were rolling and fighting in the back seat. Esther opened the car door, administering whacks at random. "Can't you stop that long enough to say hello to Aunt Bernadine? Alma, honey! How's our working girl? My goodness, you've grown tall and skinny." Esther smelled, as she always did, of anise seed and Listerine.

By the time Billy Jean came rattling back in the pick-up, they had about finished transporting the last of the suitcases and boxes of cakes and loaves of French bread into the kitchen. Aunt Bernadine rushed joyously around the kitchen, making coffee and heaping platters with cinnamon rolls and coffee cake.

"Hungry, Alma?" Bill always spoke at bellow pitch. But she slipped away to take the children out to the field where Bobby was with the men.

By four o'clock the next day she was already looking down the road for Roger's car, although they never came for her before supper. It seemed the roar of jokes and shouts had been going on for weeks.

That morning she and Billy Jean had tried to sneak off swimming—she might even have told Billy Jean, someone must be told—but the children set up a howl to come along, and Billy Jean refused. "I'm not about to be responsible for all four of them. You remember that day with Bobby. Besides, my period's coming."

Alma had felt herself scalded with a hot shame. As if Billy Jean could see in her face that she herself was never going to have a period—that right that minute inside her a baby was growing, getting bigger every day. She somehow had to say, as casually as she could, "I think mine's coming too, as a matter of fact."

When Roger and Dee finally did drive in, it still seemed like she'd never get away. Charlie had to corner Alma for an awkward goodbye—he'd been out in the fields irrigating all day Monday too; as usual, they'd seen nothing of each other except at mealtime. All the children had to be kissed. She held Bobby to her as if he were a talisman, before thankfully getting into the back seat. The silence when they drove off was heavenly.

"Ernie ought to put in some soybeans. He don't need all that alfalfa for his herd." At the end of a day with Dee, Roger, who said so little, was often loosened up enough to talk to Alma, almost to rattle on. "How many is he milking now?" Such a question was a gesture of good will toward her, she knew that, and answered him with as much detail as she could.

"So now your dad's back. Well, we'll have to hope for the best." But Dee dropped that. "You look tired. Did you have a good time, baby?"

"I guess so. With the Hinkels there's so much noise." She would tell Dee when they got home, get it over with. But when they pulled up in front, Dee didn't get out. "Roger and me are running over to the Taverna for a beer, honey. You get along to bed; I'll see you in the morning." Dee's mouth had worn through her lip gloss; she looked awfully tired herself.

Alma thought about it while she ran her hot bath. Dee spent so much time with Roger, let other things go. Lately she had neglected her friends shamefully—everything was for Roger. As much as a woman her age could be, she was probably in love with him. At least, with her pills and everything, her mother knew how to conduct a love affair. If only she had clued Alma in. If only she had just once considered the possibility of sex for her; but no, she was Dee's "baby." But it was no good blaming her mother for what had happened. That *was* babyish.

"Alma." All Tuesday morning she knew Wilma had something to tell her. Now, taking advantage of Mr. Gladburn's run down to the post office, she had dragged Alma outside. "Have you seen Howard this weekend?"

Wilma seemed to know already what the answer would be.

"No, I stayed in town. And last weekend at Oakley," —it hurt even more saying it out loud—"he didn't even phone me out there." She didn't meet Wilma's pitying eyes. The days were endless now, especially after Nelson left with his parents for Echo Lake. She was surprised to find how much she had counted on him to get her through the terrible, silent weekend in town.

"I think I better tell you. Myrna Logan's back. Jimmy and I saw them together at Meely's Saturday night." Wilma rushed back inside, and Alma followed mechanically.

As she automatically thrust MicMacs in Styrofoam boxes, she kept thinking about a story she had read somewhere, about someone lost in the outback of Australia. This person got stranded out there, nothing around for thousands of miles, nothing but shifting sand and sterile rock and hot, red skies. Utterly cut off from the rest of the world. No water, no way to survive. She remembered how very hard it was for this person to adjust to the idea that there was no hope of rescue.

She stood at the counter with her calculator and pad at the ready, the rest of the story coming back to her. This person, who later had written it all up in the book, had survived by meeting an aborigine who had shown him how to suck water out of the parched earth with reeds that reached underground channels. There had been water there all the time, no matter how hopelessly dry it looked on the surface. She really knew now what that outback must be like, and waiting out there for some kind of rescue. And also responsible for someone else's survival.

When she stripped for her bath that evening, she

111

thought she could detect a swelling to her belly. And all of them clucking about how thin she was getting. This time she didn't loiter in her hot bath. She knew now what she was going to do, and she did it the minute Dee left for the store.

With cold, sure fingers she dialed the Petroni number. Mrs. Petroni answered. Yes, she'd send one of the children out to the loading platform for Howard. Alma waited, thinking of nothing at all. Even hearing his voice didn't interfere with her concentration.

"This is Alma." She could feel his surprise, his tensing defensively, at the other end of the line. "I've got to see you right away." More silence. She would have to go on, keep saying it, until she made him come to her. "I know Myrna's back, but I've got to see you. You know where I live, in town." She waited, pushing against the wall with her bare feet, leaving wet smudges; she'd been in such a hurry she had dried herself carelessly.

She heard him exhale, as if he were sighing. "Righto. I'll be over around eight tonight."

"Thank you," she whispered, not realizing for a second that she had already put the receiver back on the hook, nor that she had covered her face with her hands. "Oh thank you, thank you."

nine

"YOU LOOK TIRED AGAIN TONIGHT, BABY. BET-ter go to bed." After supper Dee had started work on the skirt she was making.

Alma clicked off the television as casually as she could. "I'm going out for a few minutes. Howard Bab-cock's dropping by."

"Good. I've been wanting to meet that boyfriend of yours." Dee bif a thread in two with a little snap.

"Well, I wasn't going to have him come in." There was no need for them to meet. He wasn't her boyfriend, just an accidental father-to-be.

Dee frowned. "And why, may I ask, can't I meet this fancy-dancy Babcock boy? Only your Oakley relatives good enough for him?"

"No, Dee, it's not that." Dee was so touchy about being from a family like the Jenkins. "All right, all right. I'll bring him in." Of course she'd have her way. But what did it matter now what Howard thought of her and her mother? She waited by the screen door, willing the next car to be his. It was, and she ran down the walk.

"You'll have to come in and meet my mother."

Without a word he got out of the car. Beside her

once more—but only because she had demanded it. Miserably, she led him inside.

"This is Howard Babcock." She saw him taking it all in, as he had done that time before, a silent comment on the ruffled lamp shades, the flouncy chair skirts, Dee's collection of ceramic animals marching across the mantel and windowsills. Dee liked color; maybe it was too flashy. A sudden wave of dislike for him swept over her as he glanced so coolly around their living room.

She was glad Dee didn't get up from the sewing machine. "It's a working day tomorrow for Alma. See that she's home by ten-thirty." Dee wasn't about to let a Babcock think he impressed her one little bit. It was one for their side.

"This won't take long. Just go park somewhere," she commanded when they got outside. She was aware that she was deriving some faraway pleasure from giving him an order, and not caring what he thought. "We've got to talk."

Howard nodded. "I thought you might have heard that Myrna's back."

"I heard. But I knew all along I wasn't your girl." She had forgotten how beautifully shaped his hands were, that special male smell of him—she hadn't counted on that. Her heart filled with panic.

He didn't answer, driving on until they were at the far end of the golf course. He parked and reached for her hand. "I'm not sorry that we did what we did. I should be, but I'm not." His smile was all for her, but sad, regretful, a little ashamed, in spite of what he said. She looked the other way, and tried to keep her thoughts in order.

"I knew it was all wrong for a serious girl like you," Howard went on. "And believe me, if I hadn't had such a rotten summer up 'til then, I wouldn't have done it. I would have known better. I want you to understand that. But with Mother folding so spectacularly, and Myrna splitting on me—I was really down." She watched as he dug in his pants pocket for matches, a gesture that she knew so well. She clamped her hands between her knees to stop the shaking as he talked. "I was so down, you've no idea. But now she's back, and I think we've finally got it together."

"You and Myrna. Have finally got it together," she repeated idiotically.

"She's going to go to the University of Denver, see. And I'll be there at Denver High. Yeah, my uncle's putting our house up for sale and everything. A lot has been happening since I saw you last. I really did mean to give you a call. . . . You see, my mother's decided to stay in Denver. She's rented a house for us there already. We're turning over a new leaf, she says; she's making a fresh start. All that malarky." He gave her that teasing, intimate smile.

Alma clutched the door handle for support. "You're moving away?"

"Off to Denver—how do you like that for action? As long as Myrna's there—you must think I'm the pits, always talking about her. Alma, you'll always be something special to me. I'll think of you and this secret summer we had."

"Summer's going to be over. It won't be summer anymore." What a cornball thing to say. The pressure in her heart was building so she was almost afraid Howard could see it, bulging painfully out from under her ribs.

"And I haven't even asked you about yourself, your plans."

"I . . . I . . ." She moved closer to the car door. "I

guess I don't have any plans." She discovered she was whispering.

Howard slid over and put his arm around her. "I won't forget you, Alma. It was special, having a chance to get to know you."

"We've always been at school together." A great weariness was dragging at her.

"You know how it is. I've always been in the same crowd, from kindergarten on. In classes with you, sure, but I never got to know you. I always wanted to see what it would be like with someone—well, 'outside,' you might say."

"So now you know." He didn't know anything. Whatever happened to her it couldn't touch him, not Howard Babcock. She tried to bestir herself. "In some ways, one in particular, I'm more different than you think, all right." That incomparable face, the curling hair on his collar—it all had nothing to do with her; she could see that so clearly now. Because he didn't love her. He was and always would be out of her reach. Even his mother's drinking was in no way related to Charlie's drunks. A feeling of such intensity that it frightened her possessed her. She could never, never have him.

"Yeah? Well, if you ever need anything . . ."

"What could I possibly need that you could give me?" The terrible sorrow went on filling up inside her.

Howard tried a laugh. "I guess if you ever needed help, or money, or something."

"Like for an abortion." It was as if two other people were talking, somewhere else. She bent to pick a thread from the frayed edge of the upholstery.

"Thank God that doesn't come in to it. But I want you to know I'm grateful. Hey, I could have fallen in love with you. There's something about you. Shy little

Alma, and only me knowing how you really are."
Again he smiled that complete, heart-rending smile.
"You may feel kind of mad now, but someday you're
going to look back on this differently. You don't realize how you've changed."

"Neither do you." But he didn't hear her whisper.

"You've turned into a real woman this summer.
What we did . . . I'd say it was a real growth experience for you. And me too," he added quickly, politely.

"That's it, all right, especially for me." Suddenly she
exploded into laughter, high and cackly. "A real growth
experience, Howard!"

"What's the joke? Let me in on it, too."

"You're in on it, all right. Why do you think I
wanted to see you?" Her heart began to beat deafening-
ly, like a drum roll in her ears. "I'm pregnant, Howard.
I'm going to have your baby."

He slumped back. "You couldn't be! How could you
get pregnant? Nobody needs to get pregnant!"

"You should have done something, then," she said
sullenly.

"You said you were okay, after the first time! I
thought you went on the pill after that; you told me
you wanted it so much! Oh God. If my uncle hears of
this . . . but I'll come up with the money somehow.
Oh God, now I do feel guilty."

"It was my fault just as much as yours," she said
stiffly. "But I had to tell you because it's your problem,
too." She had rehearsed these words so often they had
to be used.

"Have you told anyone else, your girl friends, your
mother—that's the reason she was so shirty with me?"

She shook her head. "I tried, but I didn't tell anyone. I couldn't believe it. I didn't think I could get
pregnant just like that! It's awful being so scared all

117

the time, you just don't know." She still sat stiffly, icy tears slowing stinging down her cheeks, and knew it wasn't just the terror of being pregnant; it was also the unmentionable pain of wanting him so much and losing him so quickly, so finally. "I was so afraid to tell you."

"But that was dumb; of course I'll help you. What kind of a rat do you think I am?"

"You will?" She scarcely noticed she was wiping her wet nose on the back of her hand, great waves of relief sweeping over her. "Oh, Howard." She allowed herself to lean against him, hardly daring to believe his words. "I hoped—I knew, you'd know what to do."

"Of course I know. You get yourself up to Planned Parenthood in Delesto—as fast as your pregnant little legs will carry you. I'll drive you up if you want me to; you make the appointment. Tomorrow. The faster you have it done the better. No one but us and the doctor will ever know." He kissed the top of her head.

"You mean have an abortion." Her lips were icy again; but she had known he would say that.

He stared at her. "You're not thinking of having the baby? Don't be stupid, Alma!"

"But I don't think I can do that—have an abortion, you know."

"Nothing to it. You can probably have it taken care of right there in the doctor's office. I'm sorry as hell you'll have to go through it, but you've got no choice."

"I could go away somewhere. To the city? One of those places where you can stay and finish school, and they help you with the baby—until you can get a job." How much easier it would be if he would help her plan this, write to her, visit her on weekends. But he was going to Denver. She looked at him helplessly.

"Oh no. No, you don't! I'm not about to become a father."

Almost choking, she blazed out, "Dear old Myrna wouldn't be too happy about that, would she?"

He shook her shoulder, but gently. "Leave her out of this. Now come on. You're not going to have the baby, Alma."

She couldn't speak.

"I'll do everything I should to help you. I'll get the money you need, somehow; I'll drive you up there. There's no other way. Are you crazy?"

"I could go away somewhere, and then give it up for adoption when it's born." That would be even worse. She knew she couldn't go on living, separated in two pieces like that, knowing that she had abandoned her baby to grow up without her.

"You can't do that. You can't make me a father. Alma, I'm only seventeen years old!"

"Forget it, forget it. Just forget I said anything. Maybe it's all a mistake. Howard, please, please, take me home!"

He bucked the car into reverse at once, and roared back to her house. But when the car came to a stop, she instinctively turned to him again, and they fell into each other's arms.

"Make that appointment tomorrow. Maybe you aren't even pregnant, but if you are . . . do it for me. Please, Alma, please!"

She pulled away without answering and darted up the steps, nose streaming. After he drove away she still waited on the porch, trying to compose herself. A hot little wind lifted and rustled the sycamore leaves. Just this last week the growing season had stagnated into August heat; they were in the heaviest time of harvest now.

There was a note on the kitchen table. Roger had come by after all. "Don't wait up. Charlie called—disappointed you weren't here. Got back on at Pacific Peaches."

She made herself register that that was good news. Money from all sources would be needed. She didn't know, she would have to find out how much it cost to stay at one of those homes for pregnant girls. It might even be free. If only Dee would see for herself, and not have to be told outright. She took her bath, scalding hot out of habit, and sat waiting in the wing chair, not turning on the television. She had no idea how long she sat there. At last a car door slammed, and Dee ran lightly up the porch steps.

"You're still up! Good, I was going to wake you, anyway. Baby, I've got news!"

"Me too, Dee. There's something I've got to tell you."

"Well, look, look! Did you ever see anything as big as that!" On Dee's outthrust hand was a great rock of a diamond, flashing rainbows under the lamp. "It's happened; finally it's happened! Roger and me are going to get married in November."

Alma couldn't take it in. "You are? You're marrying Roger?"

"Honey, what else do you think has been going on? He was so soured on family life—but now! He wants me to quit my job; you know he's loaded—all kinds of property besides the ranch. Wait 'til you see the house we're going to live in—a great big private room and bath for you. Oh honey, aren't you going to congratulate me?" In her excitement she even hugged Alma to her.

"Oh, I do, Dee; of course I do. I hope you'll be very happy, you and Roger."

"You too, honey; you'll be part of it. He's such a sweet guy. Just right for me, and he's finally broken down and admitted it. Honeymoon in Hawaii—how about that. And the wedding—I've got it all planned; I want you to be my bridesmaid." Dee's face shown like Bobby's; she was all but jumping up and down with delight. She flung off her blouse. "A big wedding—no sneaking off to Reno for us. We're going to be married in the Methodist church—Ernie'll love that! A reception at that country club. The whole works. You're going to be my only attendant; I thought deep rose—so pretty on you."

"Dee! I can't be in your wedding." She looked down at her tight knuckles and made herself say it fast, all of it, get it out. "By November I'm not going to look too sharp in a bridesmaid's dress. Dee,"—she lifted her eyes—"I'm pregnant."

Dee opened her mouth and then collapsed onto the sofa, like someone in a silent movie getting it right in the stomach. "Pregnant," she whispered. "My God. A baby like you." She glared at Alma, as if she had been ambushed. "That smartass Babcock boy, isn't it? He looks just the type. Well, what does he have to say about this?"

"He says for me to get an abortion. And he's moving away, to Denver."

"Rotten little whelp!" Dee sat back, as if still trying to take it in. "And I thought I had the news tonight. You sure took the wind out my sails. Oh, this is a fine mess. Don't cry, baby, that never helped. It'll be all right. I'll make us some tea." She called from the kitchen. "How many days overdo are you? Like as not you're just a little late."

Alma felt more released at every word. They were talking intimately at last, she and her mother. She should have told her before; she understood. "It never came at all last month. I thought maybe I was just skipping. It'll be twelve weeks next Thursday."

"Twelve weeks!" Dee came to the kitchen door. "How could you let it go on so long without telling me?" Her face blazed with anger now.

"I couldn't tell you," Alma flashed back, surprising herself. "You think I'm such a baby! You wouldn't believe that I could fall in love, too. Like sex was just for you—not me. Well, it wasn't." Her voice trailed off sullenly. "Well, how could I tell you? You always treat me like a baby." Now great, painful sobs shook her. She slid lower in the big chair, aware that what she was saying shouldn't be said, but saying it anyhow. "I knew all the time about you and Roger; I knew you were having sex. But you always pretended, you always thought I was too dumb to know anything. Well, I wasn't such a baby as you thought, but—oh Dee, I don't know what I'm saying." She lay on the floor with her head in the chair, shaking and weeping. "Don't be mad at me!"

Dee knelt down beside her. "I'm not mad at you. Please don't cry. It'll be all right. And it *is* my fault. I should have told you, been honest about Roger and me. But I was scared you wouldn't understand, think I'm cheap. I know what people around here think of Jenkinses." Alma knew that Dee's family had been large and poor, before and after they all moved to Oregon, the town's only welfare cases. "I should have told you!" Alma could feel the effort it took her to say that. "But I just couldn't. Just freeze up, every time. Isn't that crazy? My mother could never talk to me about . . . sex . . . either. Couldn't bring herself to say word one. I always meant to sit you down and tell you, when the time came. When you started going out, I told myself I would, but I just couldn't do it." Her voice broke and

Alma saw tears rolling down her cheeks. She had never seen Dee cry before. "I should have taken better care of you."

It was unbearable to see Dee cry. "That's crazy. It's my own fault. I *knew*—but I just never expected to be doing that, making love."

"That's what I mean," Dee murmured brokenly. "That's what I should have told you."

"Come on, Dee, don't cry like that. Hey, where's the tea?"

"What a pair," Dee said shakily later, as they sat sipping the tea together.

Alma felt giddy with relief, and yes, happiness, she realized. They had never been so close, Dee and her. With her mother on her side, there was nothing to worry about. Only the logistics remained, and Dee could solve those easily. The long nightmare was over.

Her mother put down her cup. "Now, let me think. Tomorow I'll ask for Friday off, and we'll go to that Planned Parenthood clinic in Delesto, get the hospital date set. I don't know . . . three months. You're sure about the dates?"

"Yes, Dee." She answered meekly. It had started that very first time, she was sure of it. In the orchard there, where Howard held her so gently and whispered, *Do you want me to show you?* What an ignorant dumb bunny she had been that long, long-ago night. But a spark of a baby had been lit, just the same.

"I hope you haven't told any of your girl friends? Oh God, you haven't told Bernadine—no, of course you wouldn't; Ernie would have driven you off the place, if he knew. Well, it's not the end of the world," she said firmly. "They might even be able to do it Friday, even this late, right there in the office. No one needs to ever know a thing."

She looked at her mother, dumbly. Dee had taken charge. She would get her an abortion, and the baby would be wiped out of existence as if it had never been conceived in the first place. That was how to think of it. Now Dee was saying that, thank God, abortions were not illegal; there was nothing to an abortion anymore. "Ten years ago—five even—we would have had to scrape together every cent we could lay our hands on, and go somewhere, take your life in your hands, some filthy butcher in a back alley." Dee stopped, frowning, as if remembering something she didn't intend to remember. . . . "Well, forget that. There won't be a thing to it. You'll be back here the next day probably, and no one the wiser. Except you, I hope. And we'll just let Mr. Babcock pony up the cash to pay for it—that's the least he can do. You sure you didn't tell anyone else?" Dee couldn't seem to stop talking. She smoothed and smoothed Alma's hair, as if after this she too felt closer; she was free to touch and caress her more, now.

"No one but him. Dee, I'm really sorry to ruin your news with this." She was beginning to feel very, very tired. She just couldn't think anymore tonight.

"Don't worry about it. I've nailed Roger at last, and a little thing like a pregnant daughter isn't going to change that." She led the way into the bedroom.

Alma got silently into her bed as if, as Dee assumed, everything was settled. She had told, at last, and Dee was going to take care of her. Everything was going to be just the same as it was before. No Howard, of course, or his baby, but she must not think about that. It was all to be erased; she had been rescued. Now that she was safe, and it didn't matter anymore, she lay there in the dark and knew that she was bleeding—but only in her heart.

At last she got up and went to her mother's bed. "Dee. Wake up." She shook her gently.

Dee groaned and rubbed her eyes. "What's going on? Now what?" She switched on her lamp.

"I can't do it. I'm sorry to wake you, but I thought I better tell you. I can't get an abortion. I don't want one. I mean, I can't get one."

She had Dee's complete, wide-awake attention now. "What do you mean, you can't get one?"

"I can't do that. Dee, if I could, I'd do what you want."

"What do you mean, you can't?" Dee's little black eyes were shooting sparks.

"It's alive in there, the baby. I can't just kill this baby. Don't make me do that!"

"Now hold on a minute. Just a minute. In the first place, it's legal so that means it's right. I wouldn't ask you to do anything wrong! Why, right now it's just a little glob of sludge. You're acting hysterical. It's not a real baby yet."

"Dee, I've seen pictures. By this time they're forming. This film we have every year in phys ed—"

"Honey, you are something else. I think your mind's been affected. Even the law says you're wrong!" Dee's cheekbones were as red as if she'd just applied bright red spots of blusher. "You're crazy."

Alma clenched her fists. "I saw pictures. Even at four weeks the baby's formed a head. It has little shoulders." Tears spattered and dropped on the blanket. "It's already started. I can't do it. I can't do it! I'll go to that place, see the doctor, do everything you want, except that. Don't make me, Dee, don't make me! I'll find one of those homes for unmarried mothers, and when it's born I'll give it up for adoption if I can't take care of it." But even as she said it she knew she'd never, never be able to sever herself in two like that.

Dee sat upright in bed, her black brows twitching. "Your baby growing up, our own flesh and blood, among strangers? Someone else bringing up my grandchild! Oh no you don't. When my grandchildren are born, you're going to be settled in a nice home, and by God, I'm going to be around to enjoy them. They're going to be in their own family where they belong. Get that idea out of your head right now. You're not going to have any baby."

"Dee, I didn't mean for all this to happen. I just didn't know."

"You certainly didn't." Dee's glare was as icy and scornful as if they hadn't talked and cried together a little while ago. "But now it's time for you to show some sense." She lay back down in bed. "Baby, we've got to get some sleep." She turned to take a look at her ring, in it's blue velvet box, carefully placed in the middle of a clean handkerchief on the night table. "It'll look different in the morning." She waited until Alma had gotten back in her own bed before she turned off the light and said again, "You'll feel better in the morning."

ten

THEY OVERSLEPT THE NEXT MORNING, AND rushed around with tight faces. Dee didn't speak as she made the coffee and set out the cornflakes. They had never fallen out to this extent before, never.

Just as she was leaving, all set in her red-and-white checked jacket, red pants, red patent handbag under her arm, Dee said, meaningfully, "I'm going to make our appointment at Planned Parenthood, soon as they open."

Alma bent lower over her bowl, and her stomach lurched. How could things be worse than ever?

"It's for your own good." Dee's voice softened. "I've been awake, most of the night it seems, thinking about this. You're too young to have your life ruined because of one stupid mistake."

Alma could say nothing. She would inflict terrible pain on Dee as well as Howard by having this baby. Everybody would suffer if she didn't let it be taken away. She rinsed the dishes and sat like a robot, waiting for Dilly's mother, their faithful chauffeur, to honk.

All day she felt that she worked in a vacuum. After their shift, Dilly asked her to come home with her to hear her new Crystal Gayle tape, and Mrs. Meyer asked her to eat with them. "You haven't had supper with us for weeks."

Alma telephoned home, hoping against hope that Dee would have gone out already, but she was there.

Her voice sounded hard as ice; she hadn't given an inch. "The appointment's set for nine-thirty the day after Labor Day—the best they could do. Now I'm going to stay out at Roger's tonight;"—at least it was no longer necessary for her to pretend she didn't sleep with him—"I'll see you after work, tomorrow." She hung up with a decisive click.

As they sat down to eat, Dilly's mother reached over and felt her forehead. "You're so pale, Alma. You haven't looked well lately."

"Oh, I'm okay. I've been having these stomach attacks, sometimes." It was a dumb thing to say, sure to make Mrs. Meyer more suspicious. After that, Alma did her best to join in the laughter and talk at the table. Maybe Dilly wouldn't be allowed to have her over anymore. A pregnant friend—the Meyers weren't going to be overjoyed about that. She didn't have much appetite for the fried chicken.

After supper, Mrs. Meyer called her into her bedroom. "You and Brother go ahead with the dishes, Dilly. I want to show Alma the quilt your grandmother sent." She closed the door and took the quilt down from the cedar closet. It was for Dilly's hope chest.

"Although I hope marriage is a good long while away for her. Oh, Mike's a lovely boy, but . . . she tells me you've been dating Howard Babcock." Mrs. Meyer pushed at her stringy hair. There was a new note in her voice. Whatever was wrong, Alma had moved up socially.

She couldn't think what to say. "Not anymore," she said at last. "Well, I better be going now."

Mrs. Meyer took no notice of that. "He's had a troubled life, that kid. But you know what a fine old family the Babcocks are." She wasn't about to let Alma go until she got the story on her and Howard. In her haphazard way, Mrs. Meyer usually got to the bottom of things.

"The Babcocks are moving to Denver; I guess you know, Mrs. Meyer. Howard's mother is there already." She began to edge toward the door.

"Sit down, Alma. I wanted to have a little talk. You've been looking miserable, for weeks. Is something bothering you?"

Alma looked up to deny everything and faltered. It was hard to lie convincingly to Dilly's mother. How many Band Aids had she applied to Alma's knees over the years? How many times had she let them turn her kitchen upside down to make cookies, or drove them all over town to find the materials for their Bluebird projects, gone with them on the weekend cookouts? She had always bent over backward to make Alma feel that "not having much" in the way of family or money didn't matter; she was a perfectly fine best friend for Dilly.

"If something's bothering you, you know you can tell me."

"Oh yes. Everything's okay, though." Alma hazarded a kind of smile. She looked down again to the carpet and tried repeating more forcefully, "Really, everything's just great. Of course I'll miss Howard." At the sound of his name she had to stop. She looked up again, and saw in Mrs. Meyer's eyes that she suspected; she was reading it on Alma's own face. From some fuzzy distance she could hear a small voice, her's apparently. "I'm pretty sure I'm pregnant."

Dilly's mother sighed sadly. "I was so afraid that was it. Have you told Howard?"

She didn't want to answer. "Well, he's got another girl, you know—Myrna Logan—and she was away this summer. Now they're all moving to Denver, besides."

"Have you told your mother? Under the circumstances, I'm afraid you wouldn't get much help from poor Howard. Oh, you foolish, foolish child."

From her faraway place, Alma wondered just which circumstances were being referred to. The fact that his mother drank? That he had a girl already? He was moving to Denver? That he was only seventeen—"I'm not about to become a father"? Any one of those circumstances would seem to do.

Miserably, she wrapped her fingers around the fringe of the heirloom quilt. "She wants to take me up to that Planned Parenthood place in Delesto."

"Of course it frightens you. But it won't be so bad; I'm sure your mother's told you that. If it does turn out you're pregnant, they can take care of it very easily."

"That's what she says." She burst out with, "But you see, I can't let them do that. It's alive, that baby! I can't let them kill it."

"Child, child! What a gruesome thought. No wonder you've been going around looking like death warmed over! A twisted idea like that in your mind. You're thinking of it as if it were a real baby. It's not like that. Right now, if you're really pregnant, it's no more than a little lump of cells. That lump will turn into a real baby, though, if something isn't done."

Alma bit her lip and looked down. What would be the point of telling Mrs. Meyer of her abiding knowledge of that baby, a real baby inside her. "That's what Dee says."

"Of course! You don't have to worry about it being wrong. You can be sure it's the legal, ethical thing to do. Why, Alma, a girl as young as you are, sixteen and four months . . ." Mrs. Meyer could hardly forget the exact date of her birthday. She had arranged more joint birthday parties for her and Dilly, a week older, than could be counted on both hands. "A girl your age isn't physically ready for childbirth."

"But I can't kill my baby." She didn't mean to sound sullen, stubborn, but it came out that way.

"You mustn't think of it like that. It's not a person, with a human personality." A pinched look came over Mrs. Meyer's face. "My dear, life is hard sometimes. No one wants an abortion, but this baby shouldn't be born. You've no idea of the grief that could be. Your poor mother—and Howard has some rights in this. You must realize what's best for everyone, and then just do it."

"An abortion's not what's best for the baby."

Mrs. Meyer ran her hands through her hair and shook out the quilt she had just folded to put away. "You must think of the consequences. Surely it's not right to ask your mother to take on bringing up your baby? And your father . . ." She let that go. "Alma, it would be a tragedy. Why, your whole life is ahead of you."

They could hear Dilly and her brother scuffling out in the kitchen. Mrs. Meyer put the quilt away again and slipped her arm around Alma. She cleared her throat and seemed to speak with even more emotion. "There is another way. Have you thought of having the baby and giving it up for adoption? These days Caucasian babies are in great demand."

"I couldn't do that, Mrs. Meyer! All the rest of my life I'd be worrying about him. What if they didn't take good care of him, and I wouldn't even know?"

"There is that, of course." Mrs. Meyer seemed about

to say something and then sighed again. "All the more reason to listen to your mother. Have you told the girls? No?" Mrs. Meyer seemed relieved to hear that. "I wouldn't say anything about it, just yet. You might not even be pregnant, you know." She said that last almost pleadingly, and then added briskly, "But I must scold you for making yourself sick with these perverted notions. You have the right to an abortion these days, and you should be thankful. Now don't torment yourself with any more neurotic imaginings. There now, lecture over. You come see me after your appointment. Promise?"

Luckily, the hubbub in the kitchen was turning into a full-scale fight. Under cover of it, Alma called goodbye to Dilly and rushed out. She ran down the street as happen tomorrow, when she had to tell Dee that she wasn't asking for Tuesday off? The baby had to stay there, growing in its nest, and get born. It was part of life already. Aunt Bernadine would understand that; she would know that the baby had to be born now, come what may. But Aunt Bernadine couldn't help her, because of Uncle Ernie. She scuffed along under the sycamore trees, the leaves already drying and yellow, rustling on the branches. She would have to say another— possibly she already had—the really last good-bye to Oakley. When he heard, Uncle Ernie wouldn't even want Aunt Bernadine or Billy Jean to come to visit her. But Alma knew she could always count on their sympathy. There didn't seem to be much else to count on from anyone. Except an abortion. That's what they all wanted from her. How could she escape it on her own? At the thought of what was ahead, fighting them all, finding one of those places where she could go have the baby away from everyone, up in the city—it all seemed too much.

By the time she got home, she realized she was crying. Tiredly, she wiped the tears away with her forearm, then looked up the steps.

"Alma, sweetheart. I've been setting here since six o'clock. Don't you or Dee ever come home from work?" Charlie got up from the chair behind the vine.

"I stayed over at Dilly's for supper. Did you get your job back?" But she could tell by the way he swaggered into the house that that's what he had come to tell her.

"Took me on before I had a chance to ask. Billy Jean's going to drive me back and forth; I figure she could make a little pocket money that way." Charlie had lost his driver's license in the last binge, and he didn't have a car anyway. "She's sure peeved at her dad because he wouldn't let her work this summer, or go out with boys." He stopped, as if he'd been thinking about this. "You've got a boyfriend now, haven't you?" He peered at her, taking in the tear-smeared face.

She tried to smile. "I did have. He's going away, you see, Dad. But I did have." She was going to cry again if he didn't stop looking at her like that, as if something were breaking inside him, too.

"Honey, you've got to tell me what's wrong. If you don't tell me, how can I make it right for you?"

"Nobody can make this right. Seems to get worse all the time. I told Dee, but that's not any good." She looked down at the table top. She was going to tell him, too, she could feel it coming. Confessing pregnancy seemed to get easier with practice. "Now I've got to fight her, too. There's no one on my side."

Charlie's face seemed to get bigger; his voice was husky with emotion. "Why, darlin'. I'm on your side, you know that."

Alma got up to open the door. The evenings were warmer than ever, even though it was practically September. He was going to be very shocked, far more than Dee or Mrs. Meyer had been. Suddenly, an eerie feeling came over her. She knew exactly what she was going to say, and what he was going to say. There was a way!

"I'm in trouble, Dad. Big trouble."

The color drained from Charlie's eyes; he wiped his scarred lip uneasily. "You got to tell me what it is. That boy? By God, if he's hurt you . . ."

"He's not involved—anymore. I'm going to have a baby, Dad." She felt herself turning dark, shaming both of them with the knowledge of what she, his bragged about daughter had done. There was an unbelievable silence in the room.

"That miserable scum!" Charlie got up and then sat down again, as if bewildered by his own anger.

"Dad, it wasn't his fault. Just forget about him. He's leaving town; I've got to deal with it on my own."

"Leaving town! We'll see if he's leaving town." But to her relief, he switched targets. "You tell her about this? What does Dee say?" It was as if he was trying to gain time, trying to postpone having to come to grips with it.

"She wants me to go up to Delesto, to that clinic, and get an abortion." She debated briefly about announcing Dee's marriage news. No, one sorrow at a time. That blow could be dealt out to him later.

"That slimy no-good is going to pay for this, I'll tell you that much."

"He wants to give me the money; he's offered already. It's not fair to blame him—please, just forget all about him." She had to do the same; the baby, Howard's son, was the important one now, with only her to look out for him.

Charlie sighed. He looked older, all the summer health had drained right out of his face. "I hear it ain't dangerous anymore, doing it in the hospital. What else can you do, honey? I'm sure sorry. I figured something was wrong the minute I got back." Awkwardly, he reached for her hand. "I'm sure sorry."

"Dad, if I let them do that . . . I can't do it. Of course I didn't want a baby, but now it's there." He had to see what she had just seen, that he could help. "Dad, please help me. I could manage if you'd stand by me. Listen, we could rent a place, you and me, and you could stay at your job, maybe get on their maintenance crew and have work all winter. And I'd keep on working. Dad, don't let them make me do it. Dee's going to make me do it."

He rocked her in his arms. "Dee don't have all the say. They can't force you to have one of those operations, if you don't want it. I've got something to say about this, too."

Alma closed her eyes; her whole body sagged like a sigh of relief. He would take care of her; of course he would save her—and the baby. It was supposed to turn out this way all along. She tightened her arms around his neck. "Dad, would you really help me? If you're on my side, I know I can do it." It was going to be all right after all. Her tears fell like forgiveness—for herself, Howard, everybody.

He rubbed his chin, thinking aloud. "Fella down at the plant today, telling me his son-in-law is moving to San Jose—hadn't sublet his place yet. I'll ask about that first thing tomorrow. Don't you cry, darlin'. It's going to be all right. We'll show her." He was grinning, as delighted as Alma with the way it was going to be. "You don't need that operation. I'll be taking care of you now."

Alma stood up, still holding his hand. He had given her back her old self. There was a future for the two of them, together, as they had once been so long ago. "Dad! I should have known you'd help me." The tears kept coming as she rummaged around the kitchen for cookies. When they got their own apartment, she would bake beautiful homemade ones for him.

Charlie lolled at ease now, teetering on the back legs of his kitchen chair. "That apartment, he said it was on Ventura Street, overlooks the river."

"Sounds great. Is it furnished, Dad?"

He watched as she got down the mugs and poured milk into the little pitcher. "Why, there ain't all that much we'd need. A stove—we could pick that up easy down at the Salvation Army store. Get us a table, few chairs."

"And beds. Maybe Dee would let me take mine from here." Dee wouldn't want any of this old furniture now, but just in time she remembered not to say that or she'd have to tell him why. "I can make the curtains, you know." There was so much to discuss. "Dad, when do you think we could take a look at the place?"

He got up and began to pace back and forth, taking fire from her enthusiasm. "I'll speak to him first thing in the morning. We'll need to get us a few dishes, blankets. . . . You got a piece of paper?" They bent over the list, which grew rapidly. "Of course, we'll have to be careful of money."

"I'll ask if I can stay on at MicMac's, work evenings and weekends. They pay us the minimum, Dad—not much, but it'll help. And with all you'll be making at Pacific Peaches, I know we can manage. And Dad, I think I can get some kind of Aid to Dependent Children money, later." She couldn't help blushing. "I'll go up to that place with Dee, so I can ask them about Aid money and school and things like that." A home teacher would probably visit her, like the one that went out to the spastic Douglas boy.

Charlie's eyes blazed sulpher blue points. "You just tell them up there that your Dad's going to take care of you from now on." He caught sight of the clock. "Is that right? Ten-thirty already? I got to run for it; Bradshaw's giving me a ride home; he took her in to the movie tonight."

It seemed that they had no more walked into the house, and now he had to go. He came back up the steps to tell her something else he had just thought of.

"Sooner or later we'll have to let the folks out at Oakley know, and I'll just bet Bernadine will give us a lot of stuff for the house. Have to sneak it out on the sly; old Ernie's going to scream hell's fire." He laughed and then kissed her again, solemnly. "Take care now, darlin'. I'll call you tomorrow."

Alma flew around the place, washing their cups, too excited to go to bed. Her Dad was taking charge; he would see her through, and they would be together. Dee couldn't force her to get rid of the baby now. And she wouldn't have to go away to the city, among strangers, to save it. Her Dad would take care of her. She stopped, holding a sudsy mug in midair. Maybe she would just tactfully suggest that it might be a good idea for him to start going to the AA meetings—he did that sometimes —just to make sure he'd be all right from now on.

Odd that they hadn't talked about that. But they would; she'd bring it up next time. Now they could talk about anything, she and Charlie. Of course he wouldn't start drinking. Not after all the plans they'd made, all the things they were going to do—not now when he could see how much she needed him.

eleven

THE FIRST THING ALMA DID AT MICMAC'S THE next morning was to corner Mr. Gladburn and ask if she could go on working after school started. Weekends and evening shifts?

Mr. Gladburn was pleased with such a sign of industry. "You're a real go-getter, Alma. All summer I said to my wife, 'she's the only one of the troopers who really took hold.' "

The first step of their plan—hers and Charlie's—was taken.

She mentioned that she was going to go on working to the girls as they waited for Mrs. Meyer to pick them up.

"Honestly, you're money mad," Dilly said, peering down the road at the shimmers of heat. "How can you bear to spend weekends in this hole after school starts?"

"That's not all I can bear." Alma actually felt cheerful enough to tease them a little. "I'll tell you all about it . . . one of these days."

"Tell us why you have to have Tuesday off, too," Wilma suggested. Then she blurted out, "Jimmy told me that Helen Gamboli had a big farewell party for Howard and Myrna last night."

"She invited Mike and me," Dilly admitted, with a glance at Alma. "Of course, we didn't go," she added virtuously.

It had nothing to do with her anymore; Alma soon recovered from the stab of hearing his name. She could hardly wait to get home to make herself a big submarine sandwich. All the way in the car she planned just what she'd put on it. Cheese, salami, pickles, baloney.

Dee walked in, eyes hard as her voice had been over the phone the night before. She set her overnight case down with a thud.

"I see your appetite's returned."

Alma swallowed her mouthful and decided remarks about eating for two wouldn't be well received at the moment.

"I hope you've come to your senses, baby. That appointment's for Tuesday morning."

"I'll go, Dee. Those people will help me. But I'm not going to get any abortion." Under the table she clenched her fingers into fists.

To her surprise Dee's eyes softened and filled. She sat down at the table, too, and turned the blazing ring on her finger; both of them watched the colors trembling in its lights. "Oh, honey. You can't possibly manage having a baby; you're still just a little girl yourself. And I don't want to bring it up. I can't. Roger's done his time with babies!"

"I don't need you to help me. I can do what I've got to do."

Dee moaned and put her hands to her head.

"My Dad's going to help me. He came over last night. He's got his job back, and we're going to rent a place, the two of us, and—"

"Charlie? Help you? Now I know you're out of your mind!" Dee slammed into the bedroom.

Alma turned eagerly back to what was left of her sandwich. She thought for a minute and then started slicing cheese and salami for another one.

Howard called while she was in her bath, leaving his uncle's phone number. Dee had written it out in big digits. "Aren't you going to call him? Give him the big news that you've decided he's going to be a daddy before he's dry behind the ears?" It was bad business, locking horns with Dee. But she couldn't force Alma to call him.

To her great relief, Nelson, back from his vacation at Echo Lake, dropped by after their silent, uncomfortable supper. She was waiting for Charlie's call, but the black, explosive atmosphere around Dee was unbearable. She suggested to Nelson they take a walk.

"I hear your sweetie's blowing town." Nelson looked a shade thinner. He took her hand with a new kind of confidence.

"How'd you hear that? Well, it's true." She looked up at the shreds of clouds scuttling over a very pale little scrap of moon. This was her most vulnerable time. She just had to keep herself from weakening; she couldn't afford the luxury of grieving over Howard.

Holding her hand, Nelson went on awkwardly, "Under the circumstances, we might consider that I take over his spot?"

"We might, but let's not." Alma was surprised at the sure way she knew how to deal with this. Not for anything would she hurt Nelson. "You don't want a girl the shape I'm in."

"You're going to have to explain that."

It seemed crazy to tell Nelson before she told the girls, but suddenly she wanted to. "Okay. You're going to hear, or see, for yourself pretty soon anyway." She stopped to tear off a bougainvillaea leaf to sniff, took a deep breath, her heart beating recklessly. "I'm going to have a baby."

Nelson stopped dead on the sidewalk, his eyes wide behind the big glasses. Then he wheezed out a nervous laugh. "Look, just come right out and say you can't stand me, okay? Don't stall with something as feeble as that." But he looked scared.

"Nelson, I *am*."

"Jee-eez!" It rocked him, all right. He withdrew his hand gently, as if any sudden movement might start her delivering the baby right then and there on the sidewalk. "You're absolutely the last chick I would ever expect to make that announcement. The Great Profile's work, no doubt. But of course you'll get rid of it."

"If I were, I wouldn't have needed to tell you, or anybody, would I?" She felt almost happy, astonishing him like this, talking about the baby. This was quite different from confessing pregnancy to an adult. It seemed she'd been confessing to every adult she had seen, lately.

"Let's sit down here, Alma; I've got to sort this out. For some reason, no abortion? And the father's split to Denver. There's not going to be any father around to help you?"

"Yes, there is, as a matter of fact. *My* father. We're going to get an apartment together." She had so much to tell. "My mother's getting married, and she doesn't want any part of this. But my Dad's going to help me. We're going to get an apartment together."

"You said that." He shook his big head slowly, still not used to it. "Now, I don't want to offend, but word gets around a burg the size of Oaklon, you know. I hear that your dad qualifies as the town boozer."

She winced. "He's had a drinking problem, but that's all over now. He's going to stay sober, Nelson; he's got reason to now. He knows I'm counting on him. He's got a job and everything. I'll stay on part-time at Mic-Mac's."

"Wait a minute. What about school?"

"I'll go, for a while. They'll have a home teacher come to the house—when I get too big." It was going to be embarrassing when word got around town, but she'd tough it out. Her Dad would be taking care of her. "I've got to get my diploma so I can get a real good job, to take care of my baby."

"But what happens when you can't work anymore, and your dad is laid off or, God forbid, goes off the wagon?"

"He won't, Nelson. We've worked it all out. If he does get laid off this winter, there's his unemployment insurance, and there's bound to be some welfare I can get, Aid to Dependent Children. My mother and I are going up to that Planned Parenthood place in Delesto. They'll counsel and stuff."

"Let me get this straight. You, under age and pregnant, co-starring with your dad, the well-known alkie. Between the two of you you'll go off into the sunset and raise this love child? Wow, that'll really show your mother where to get off, won't it?"

"What else can I do? You talk as if I have some other option." All her good feeling was flooding away.

"Why couldn't you give the kid up for adoption?" He looked at her sharply and then answered his own question. "No, you couldn't. I can see from here that you're not about to give up any baby you fight this hard to have."

"I didn't want a baby, you know. I shouldn't have done what I did, but I did, and it happened. So don't I have to take it from there, do what I know is right?" She felt very pregnant and scared again.

"God and the great Babcock ganged up on you. You

know, back at my old high school in Berkeley it got fashionable to get pregnant. Yeah. Status thing. All the chicks making themselves important."

Something seemed to click inside her, even as she thought that girls in Oaklon certainly wouldn't do that. She hadn't gotten pregnant on purpose. Although, she had to admit, she'd been surprisingly stupid about it. . . . But now there was no other way. She had to have Howard's baby. "I think that's awful. Sick. But this baby— I'll manage okay with my dad's help."

Nelson squeezed her hand. "I for one will be rooting for you, all the way."

She thought again about those girls in the city, deliberately having babies. And what he'd said about getting back at Dee . . . "Maybe when you do what's right, there still might be some wrong reasons for doing it mixed up in there, too? But you can't help that. It doesn't matter so much, about the wrong reasons, if you're still going to try for the right ones."

"I'm glad you cleared that up. For a minute.there I was a little confused." They both laughed, and Nelson got up and pulled her gently to her feet. "Now, bearing in mind what's ahead, and I choose the word "bearing" with care, I suggest a nourishing milkshake at Meely's."

Over their shakes they laughed and joked; Nelson was one friend she'd really need to see her through the months ahead.

"I guess your parents are going to be shocked, Nelson. I figure the baby'll be born in March; six months before it's all over."

"All over? That's when it begins." Nelson slurped up the last of his thin, low-calorie shake.

"I guess you're. right." The baby's birth was, of course, the beginning; Nelson was sharp to have pointed that out to her.

She felt sobered as she ran up the porch steps, even before she saw Dee was in, doing her nails at the kitchen table.

"Nelson took me for a shake at Meely's."

The silence emanating from Dee rolled on unbroken.

"Dee, I'm not being this way just to be mean." The phone rang out, and they both jumped.

Without saying a word beyond "hello?" Dee handed it to her. "Your wonderful father."

"Oh, I'm just fine, Dad. How's everyone out there? I bet you're calling to say you got the apartment." Dee made a sudden movement, spilling her polish remover.

Charlie's voice sounded very far away. "I just got to thinking, darlin'. Maybe you're biting off more than you can chew."

Alma swerved around so that her back was to Dee. Her heart went off its beat, out of rhythm. "I thought it was *we,* Dad, *we.*" She didn't care that Dee was listening to every word.

"Bernadine's not going to be able to do a thing to help us. Ernie won't let her; you know how he'll react."

"I don't care about that! You haven't changed your mind about us living together and everything?" She could scarcely breathe. "Dad, you're running out on me!"

"Now why you say a thing like that? You know I'll stick by you as long as I can. It's your own good I'm thinking about. You might be a lot better off if you just went ahead and had that abortion like your mother wants. And go right on with your schooling."

"Oh, Dad, you've changed your mind." The news seemed to blur her hearing as well as her sight. She clung tighter to the receiver.

"No sir. We're going to do it. Just the way you planned. I only wanted you to reconsider, for your own good. You're not crying, are you, honey? Alma, listen. There's a kid at the cannery says he's got a stove we can have for nothing. Just come and haul it off, he said. You hear that? No sir! We're going to rent that place and everything, just the way you want. You tell your mother I'm taking over."

When she hung up, she said only, "He thought I ought to think it over again. Maybe your mother's right, he said."

"Even Charlie can see good and well I'm right. He's not going to help you, honey. But I'm staying out of it; you do what you want from here on in. All these years I've done for you and done for you, tried to bring you up right. You don't have to tell me that I've gone wrong, but I tried my best. And I'm having no part of this foolishness." She flounced off to the bedroom.

There was no point any longer trying to talk with Dee. Later, Alma lay in her bed, trying to put that phone conversation out of her mind and concentrate on what they would need. Phone and water and electricity —they'd forgotten to figure those in.

It was a long while before she fell asleep. There was so much not to think about. . . . Howard hadn't phoned again. That appointment—she decided she wouldn't tell the girls or say a word about the baby to anyone, until that appointment Tuesday.

The next day a heat wave hit; time seemed stuck fast at two-thirty in the afternoon. When Alma finally did get home from work Dee was gone. There was a note, saying that she was doing a big shopping at Safeway.

Alma hoped it would be a good long while before she came back. The bad feeling between them kept on and on. Maybe after they had their appointment with Planned Parenthood, when Dee realized she wasn't going to change her mind, the air would clear. Hot as it was, she hurried to prepare herself a big pre-supper snack.

Someone knocked at the screen door.

"Billy Jean, hey, I'm glad to see you. What are you doing in town? Oh, you came for my father; he said you were driving him back and forth from his job." She wouldn't tell her yet, either. "When does he get off today?"

"He said three; I've been to the plant. He wasn't there, where I pick him up. I went in finally, and they said he'd left an hour ago. I thought he might have come up here."

The girls looked at each other. Alma put down the butter knife. The room dipped, and through the window the trees made crazy green patterns against the still sky. She bolted for the bathroom, Billy Jean dashing after her.

"What's going on in there? Are you sick? Alma!" If Billy Jean had stopped pounding on the door and yelling, she would have heard well enough that she was. Alma sat up, wiped her face and rinsed the vomit out of her mouth. She steadied herself against the cold porcelain of the sink before she got up and unlocked the door.

"You were being sick!" Billy Jean cried. "Do you think it's that summer flu again?"

"No, I don't." She looked away from her glassy white face in the mirror. "Did you go by the Beeline Bar?"

Billy Jean busied herself sponging the tiles. "Alma, I didn't dare. I didn't know what to do. Do you think he's off drinking?"

"He's off drinking, all right." She whirled around;

she would tell Billy Jean about her pregnancy—but then it came to her that maybe there would be no need. On her own she wouldn't be able to save this baby.

Back out in the living room, Alma sat down heavily. "You better go on to Oakley. I'll stay here by the phone; sometimes he phones up after he gets started." Before the night was over, he'd probably be calling. *"Now you come on down here, darlin'. Honey, I didn't aim to do it. Man don't have a chance these days. I didn't mean to leave you, Alma!"* He was going to feel so bad about it, letting her down like this. She closed away from her the scene of just two nights ago; she and her father talking, planning, the eager words tumbling out, so much for the two of them to say to each other. Before morning he would be lost, the last scattered pieces of their plans were blowing away right now.

"Hello, Billy Jean. I didn't know you were coming by."

Behind her two big brown bags of groceries, Dee peered sharply at both of them. Sensing something was in the air, she put the groceries down cautiously. "What's the matter?"

"It's Uncle Charlie." Billy Jean went on the defensive. "I was supposed to pick him up after his shift. We were just wondering where he was."

Dee brought her black brows together in a scornful line. "You can save yourself the trouble of wondering. Of course he's off drinking again. What else? Or do you think he's out renting an apartment for you, Alma?"

"You and Charlie are going to rent an apartment? Why?" Confused, Billy Jean turned to Alma.

Dee moved in swiftly. "I'm getting married to Roger Steegmuller. But don't say anything to your folks; we haven't announced it yet. So Alma thought . . . but of course it never would have worked out. You see that now, baby, it wouldn't of worked."

Alma shook her head, sinking down into her chair. "You might have known how it would turn out. I told you, honey."

"I was going to go down later to look at curtain material. Kress's having a sale." She knew as she said it how dumb it sounded. "It was too much to put on him, wasn't it?" She didn't even try to hide her tears. Poor Billy Jean looked more confused than ever.

"Here." Dee handed her a Kleenex. "It could never have been the way you had in mind."

"If Alma needs a place to live," Billy Jean said, as if struck by a happy thought, "we'd love to have her out at Oakley!"

Dee tied an apron firmly around her tiny waist. "No need. She's staying right with me. I'm taking care of her. I always did, and I intend to go right on."

Neither of them noticed that Alma's hands were pressed to her stomach, as if to protect as long as she could what was in there.

"I've got to go. You hear from him, Alma, call Mamma right away. She always gets so upset; you'd think she'd get used to it by now." Billy Jean rushed down the steps, glad to leave them.

"I got us a steak; we're going to be needing our strength." That's all Dee said, and she went ahead and fried it. Neither of them mentioned how unusual it was for Alma to sit hunched and quiet, making no move to help, before or after the meal. Alma was reminded that Dee, a relentless fighter, was also a generous winner. She was giving Alma time to get used to what was ahead.

Sitting there in the wing chair again, Alma had the crazy impression she was out among parched, colorless rocks, the hot red skies of the outback pressing down on her, the rumors of water getting fainter as she got weaker and weaker, just the barren landscape closing in.

At first she didn't hear the soft but insistent knocking at the door.

twelve

She had known it wouldn't be Charlie, but she wasn't prepared for Howard, either.

"I'd like to talk to Alma, please." He kept his eyes trained anxiously on Dee as if, without her permission, he'd turn right around and leave, without so much as a glance at Alma.

Dee snorted. "Can't harm her anymore now, can you? All right, all right. Maybe you can talk some sense into her." She stalked out of the room.

Alma got up and followed Howard out to his car, hardly aware of what she was doing. Before starting the motor, he turned and took her icy hands into his. "You never called me back."

"There wasn't any point." But, unwillingly, she found herself feasting her eyes on him. His face had tanned to a dusky apricot; he needed a haircut badly. He was not for her; she should be getting the message by now. But oh how good it was to be beside him again! "I thought you'd be packing for Denver."

"I'm packed," he answered moodily. "But I'm going crazy worrying about you. You haven't done it yet, have you?"

Alma clutched her hands together and prayed for

strength to resist, to ignore—they were all against her, she thought with a rush of anguish. Every last one of them. "Howard, leave me alone. Please go away and leave me alone."

"But I want to help. It's my problem too, remember?"

"Not anymore. You've gone back to Myrna—I'm not your girl."

He gave her that heart-twisting smile. "Somehow I keep thinking of you as my girl. My sweet, secret girl. Myrna—ah well. People can be difficult."

She hardened her heart, lips trembling, but she had to get the words out. "You're leaving. We've got to remember that."

"You won't let me help you?"

"I don't want that kind of help."

"Do what you want, then!" He started the car with a roar and drove through the warm dusk, faster and faster. They whirled past the carnival that had been set up for Labor Day weekend in the shopping center north of town. It was a big one, with a Ferris wheel, hammer whip, little cars, penny pitches. Triangular banners were hung all around the parking lot. "They always come at the end of summer," Howard murmured. Suddenly he pulled the car to the side and reversed. "Let's go to the carnival. End of summer, right? End of the line for us? Let's celebrate!"

They could do nothing else; her mood changed too, as if a light had been switched on.

As they got out of the car they heard the merry-go-round music, and to Alma it seemed as if it were calling personally to them. They walked along the mall, hand in hand, under the flags, passing the big, bubbling bouquets of helium-filled balloons bobbing pale colors against the pearly sky. She'd been granted a sudden reprieve from her troubles. Cut loose, set free. She smiled up at Howard joyously, as if she really were his girl, as if she weren't pregnant, and they weren't going to be parted forever.

They did all the rides, one after another. Swooping down the roller coaster, clinging to him, shrieking with happiness and terror, she felt they were being transported from this world. Maybe the machinery would crash and they would die together. She would have a miscarriage—the ride would never end. When it did, they hurried over to the hammer whip, as if they dared not pause—then the giant cups-and-saucers, the little cars; side by side on two purple ponies they rode the merry-go-round three times in a row, holding hands, laughing idiotically across to each other. Then they were high up in the Ferris wheel, where they seemed to hang out along with the bright, splintery stars. Rocking back and forth in the night, Alma had a premonition that this evening was something she would always remember completely, in every detail, even when she was an old, old lady. It was one of those interludes, she decided, that become timeless and so is never lost, that is always shining through the past. Knowing that, she knew too she would find the strength to do what had to be done.

The lights strung along in aisles reflected the dust as a golden haze. They ate great cones of cotton candy as they walked, stopping to throw balls at the wooden ducks and toss pennies at the next pitch. The lights began to go out; the carnival was closing. Reluctantly, they left, with the last of the crowd.

Howard drove further on and parked the car in front of a field of tall, rustling corn. At last he held her in his arms, so hard she thought she would faint with pleasure. "Tell me that you forgive me."

"It's okay," she whispered. "It's all right. You must forgive me, too." She added silently, *for what I'm going to do*.

"Forgive you? For breaking my heart by being so sweet?" Through the dark she thought she saw tears glinting in his eyes. "I don't have any peace, worrying about you. Thinking about you. I think about us now, all the time. Isn't that crazy?"

"Crazy," she agreed. "Oh, Howard."

"I don't see how I can leave you here, pregnant, and I don't see how I can't show up in Denver tomorrow, Myrna and Mother waiting—"

It was so clear to her now, what had she to do for both of them. Especially for him. She stroked his cheek. "There's nothing to worry about anymore. I'll get the abortion."

It was worth it to hear the happiness in his voice. "You will? Thank God. You don't know what a load this is off my mind." She kept her fingers crossed as he kissed her. "Write to me. We mustn't lose touch."

She lied again. "Sure. I'll write." He would be watching the mail for a letter that would never come, but that had to be. Let Myrna comfort him. . . . She swallowed her tears, smiling up at him.

It was much later when they finally said good-bye. She stood on the porch watching him go down the walk—for the last time. The night wind was beginning to stir the heavy branches of the big elms across the street. Autumn was in the air.

Late as it was, Dee wasn't back. Alma pulled on a sweater and sat waiting, rehearsing. When her mother came in, she tackled her at once. "I'm not going to get an abortion, Dee. You can't make me." Her mother said nothing. Alma faltered, but went on. "Howard thinks I am. He's sending the money, but that's all right. I'll need it."

"I'll say you will." Dee sat down heavily. "Still determined, even after the way Charlie let you down. Okay. You win. That's right, baby, you win. If she's still against it, Roger says, you've got to stop fighting her. It's her baby, he says." She tried to grin.

"Oh, Dee. Do you really mean it?"

"I usually mean what I say, don't I? I'll help you all I can, as long as it's understood him and I aren't going to bring it up. Let's get that clear right now. Okay. We'll find out Tuesday about one of those places in the city; you can go there and finish your schooling. We'll just say you've gone to stay with my sister in Oregon. I suppose everyone in town will soon know better."

Alma went over and hugged her, and Dee hugged back. Along with her relief, Alma felt shame and confusion. It wasn't right for her to put this trouble on Dee. But no matter what she did now, other people were going to suffer.

"I didn't want to make you unhappy, Dee. I didn't want you to have to get involved."

Dee smiled a queer smile. "Life's connected. Whatever you go through, your family and friends have to go through, too. I know I was being hard on you about the abortion, but it was your own good I had in mind. You know I'd fight tooth and nail for that."

"I know, I know. But I just couldn't. I can't do that."

"Roger says you shouldn't be tormented about it anymore. Let her have the baby. We can help out with the money, he says, but no way are we going to bring it up."

"Oh, no. I'll do it. I can manage."

Dee went on, as if she hadn't heard that. "We're going to get married in November, just like we planned. And I don't care if you have to wear a blanket, you're going to be my attendant."

"Oh, Dee." Alma kissed her again, but felt compelled to add, loyally, "I know Charlie would have helped me, if he could."

"Charlie was never built for crises; I tried to tell you. Now don't worry about him. They'll find him and get him back to Oakley; they always do."

She had to think then of the pain she would inflict on Aunt Bernadine and all of them at Oakley, one way or another. Because of one careless, ecstatic act. But at least she had saved her baby. He wouldn't suffer.

Tuesday afternoon, when they got back from Delesto, she called the girls, and they met at Dilly's.

"Okay, girl, give! What is it you want to tell us?"

Alma got up to test the catch on the bedroom door again, to make sure Dilly's little brother wasn't hanging around. She swore them first to secrecy. And then she told them.

Their mouths hung open in soft, round O's.

Dilly finally spoke. "We just thought all the time that it was because Howard wasn't serious. Why didn't you tell us?"

"I did tell your mother, Dilly, finally. I was so ashamed."

"You couldn't help falling in love with a rat. He is, Alma!"

"No, that's not fair. I shouldn't have been so dumb." There was one thing she had planned to be sure and say. "I learned something the hard way. Girls get pregnant. Boys don't. They can skip town." But that was mean. Was it Howard's fault that he was going to Denver? None of this would have happened if he had played fair with her, and Myrna too, in the first place. But it was too late to assign blame. "He's only seventeen, after all. That's no age to be a father."

"No age to be a mother, either." She had made them understand that there'd be no abortion. "You won't even *be* seventeen when it's born." The thought sobered all three of them.

Alma went on to tell about the plans they had made with the social worker. "Dee and Roger will drive me up next weekend. It's supposed to be a great school; they have counseling, and they teach you how to take care of the baby. You can stay there for a while after it's born, until you get a job." All alone in the big city. When it got too scary though, she would remember the baby that was going to be hers. She wouldn't be alone, ever again.

The social worker hadn't liked the way she had insisted she would keep the baby. Round-faced, with big, colorless pug features, she talked to Dee as if Alma had left the room.

"Perhaps after counseling, she'll come to see that she doesn't *need* to keep this baby, to fulfill her own emotional needs."

Dee had sat up straighter, as if stung by that. "My daughter's trying to do what's best for this baby."

"Then I'm sure she'll want to consider adoption very, very carefully," the social worker had gone on smoothly. "We always have a waiting list of excellent homes, especially for Caucasian placements."

Alma had squirmed miserably in her chair, hating the social worker for implying that she wanted the baby to play with, like a child longing for a doll to dress and feed. Calling her baby a "Caucasian placement."

Mrs. Meyer knocked and then stuck her head in the room. The girls looked stricken until Alma said. "Relax. She knows all about it, remember?" She turned to Mrs. Meyer. "I've been telling them about the home I'm going to, in the city, where I can go to school and learn how to take care of the baby and everything."

"You *are* pregnant, then?" Mrs. Meyer said sadly.

"Three months, the doctor said. Finishing the first trimester." It was silly to say it as if it were an accomplishment or something. "The cover story is that I'm staying with my aunt in Oregon." Not a word about this baby must reach Denver. She had to play fair, she said to herself sternly. She was taking full responsibility for his being born, so he was all hers, now. "You can pretend you don't know me if the gossip starts."

Wilma came over and kissed her. "Is that any way to talk to your baby's aunties?" There were tears in her eyes, and Dilly looked moved, too.

Mrs. Meyer said reproachfully, "We don't turn on our friends when they're in trouble. Alma, come out to the kitchen with me; we'll find some Cokes." They were going to have another little talk, Alma could see.

Mrs. Meyer sat her down at the kitchen table. "Did they talk to you and your mother about adoption?"

"The social worker said I'd have time to think about that. But I told her already. I won't ever give this baby up to strangers."

"People do, honey. It isn't easy, but sometimes for a young girl it's by far the best." Mrs. Meyer took a deep breath. "I did."

Alma stared.

"Dilly and her brother don't know, and of course

you won't tell them. Oh, it happened a long, long time ago, before I'd even met Dilly's father. I was nineteen. . . . In those days it was a terrible sin. The worst disgrace. But my parents stood by me and, after it was born, arranged for the baby to be adopted into a good home."

"How could you bear to give it up?"

"Because it was best for the baby," Mrs. Meyer answered simply, as she got down the glasses. "I wanted him to have a father and mother, a real home. That's why I did it."

"But wasn't it awfully hard? How could you ever forget? I mean, how can you forget your own baby?" Alma's voice went high and painful. "I don't see how you could, ever."

"You don't," Mrs. Meyer said harshly. "You never do forget, and it hurts for a long, long time. He'll be twenty-one this month. If he's alive. I don't even know that, you see. Every year on his birthday—but the first birthdays were much more agonizing." She shook ice out of the icemaker. "There are many things in life, Alma. It's all ahead of you at sixteen. You can't let one sorrow ruin it. You learn to overcome the pain. You go on."

Her baby, too, would be a boy, and she would never give him up to strangers! "I'd die before I'd give up my baby!" But even as she said it, that unthinkable solution settled in the back of her mind, like it had taken on a weight of its own.

Alma was very quiet that evening. Dee had narrowed her silverware pattern down to three: *Forever Thine, The Rose and Hart,* and *Precious Memory,* and was agonizing over the final choice. "I promised Roger I'd tell him tomorrow. Come on, honey, tell me which one. Oh, it's so hard to make decisions!"

"Okay, I'll tell you. *Precious Memory*—by a mile." Her mind was still on that talk with Mrs. Meyer. But it would be weeks, months, before she'd have to make decisions, like about her son or anything. She'd know how to handle it, when the time came.

thirteen

ALMA LOOKED DOWN AT THE TRAFFIC RUSHING by on the avenue below. The light changed, and the trucks, vans and cars lunged under and over the sprawling gray cement overpasses and underways. Fog filled in the ends of the streets. On clear days she had a nice view of the bay from her third-story room. There were so few clear days, and it was always cold in the Bay Area.

Her bags were packed, although Dee and Roger weren't due until four. Then they were going to continue right on up the coast to Seattle, Vancouver and over to Victoria, before they came back to Roger's ranch. She'd live there with them this summer, before she went away to college in Lockdale, fifty miles down the Valley from Oaklon. How she'd love being back in that warm Valley, again. Bake out her bones. She'd made Roger agree that the money was only a loan; when she got her teacher's credentials she'd pay it all back, along with what she'd already borrowed. "You get more independent every day," Dee had said when she phoned. But Alma knew that her mother, who'd always been so self-sufficient herself, thought that that was the right way to do it.

She hadn't had many visitors. And of course months ago Howard had stopped writing; she'd never answered one of his letters. Wilma and Dilly had come over during Christmas vacation, and the three of them had had a wonderful time sight-seeing in Chinatown and everything. They'd never seen her baby. Alma checked the crib; still sleeping so soundly, so sweetly.

When Aunt Bernadine and Billy Jean had come last month, it had been a real surprise. Alma had run up all three flights, breathlessly, coming in from her kitchen shift to find them already in the nursery. They were talking to Mrs. Blakely, who watched the babies while the girls were in classes or at their jobs. A baby was bellowing a blue streak—hers, of course.

"My relief was late," Alma explained, still trying to get her breath back, lifting Samantha out of her crib. She carefully picked blue blanket fuzz off her tiny mouth. "She never cries, really. She hardly ever cries at night in our room."

Aunt Bernadine held out her arms for the baby. She was all dressed up for her rare trip to the city in a new beige and brown checked polyester suit that puckered up strangely over her plump shoulders. She had new brown shoes; even her handbag was brand-new. Billy Jean seemed very cheerful. No wonder; she'd written Alma that she had a job at 4H camp for the summer, and would be out from her father's watchful eye at last. With her away, and Aunt Selma dead, and no Alma, it would be quite a different summer at Oakley.

"She's not wet." Aunt Bernadine had cuddled the baby to her big, pillowy bosom. Her face had shone with love. "No sirree! Just wanted someone to snuggle you a little, didn't you, sugar. What a little beauty. Looks more like Dee than anyone, doesn't she?"

Samantha did. She certainly didn't resemble Howard

or Alma in the slightest. It had been a difficult birth, despite all the exercises and training. Alma had had to be put out completely. When she'd awakened, the nurse had hemmed and hawed for a minute, breaking it to her gently that she didn't have the boy she had been so sure of. But once she had a glimpse of Samantha—long hair plastered against her bruised, dented face, that plump little purple body, like a fat rat—the most enormous love had welled up in her, and she knew that this was the baby she'd wanted all along, and she'd love her forever and ever.

"Little sweetheart. Oh, what a little precious she is." While she'd crooned and cuddled Samantha, now all pink and white and blonde, Aunt Bernadine had also looked over Alma. "You're awfully thin, honey. I'm afraid you work too hard."

"It'll be better when school's out. I'll have a full-time shift in the laundry then, but I won't have homework."

"Seems like there should be more help for you," Aunt Bernadine had said, shaking her head.

"I'm lucky I can stay here another year, until I'm eighteen. By then I should have things organized. A good job, an apartment, a good child-care center for her." It made her immensely weary, thinking of handling all that, even with the support the social worker would give.

"Here, Billy Jean. I know you're dying for a chance to hold her. Now, honey, I must tell you." Aunt Bernadine had looked unhappy, but determined. "We've been here forty minutes, setting in the hall waiting before they would let us in. That baby's been crying the whole time."

Alma looked angrily over at Mrs. Berkeley, now down at the other end of the room, fussing with two babies who were crying there.

162

"I don't suppose it's her fault," Aunt Bernadine went on. "Although she does move kind of slow, I think she does the best she can. Well, I had to tell you, honey. And you look so worn out. When was the last time you went out, had a little fun?"

It seemed years ago—certainly before the baby was born—but she didn't want to admit that. "I like to spend all my free time with Samantha. I get to be with her so little."

Aunt Bernadine had met her eyes. Alma knew the same thought was in both of their minds. If only she could bring Samantha to Oakley. But that was crazy. It couldn't ever be, and they both knew it.

Aunt Bernadine had won one concession. "I've had a talk with Ernie. It's hard for him to understand, you know, but I'm coming now every month to visit you. Next time I'm going to bring Bobby."

Dear Aunt Bernadine. She knew what that would mean to Alma, seeing Bobby. It was almost as good as getting to go back to Oakley.

Bernadine had also brought her latest letter from Charlie, in Reno again. "He knows you're too busy now for much letter writing. He's rarin' to come back, see his new granddaughter." Aunt Bernadine had laughed; whatever he did, Charlie never failed to please and amaze her.

When it was time for them to go, she had laid the baby gently back in Alma's arms. "Now, honey, you phone me more often. It's all settled that you're to call collect. I can't help worrying about the two of you. That babysitter," she had said again, "she moves so slow."

"Some of us have been complaining about her," Alma had tried to reassure Aunt Bernadine. "I'm pretty sure they're looking for a replacement." The doubtful look on Aunt Bernadine's face had stayed.

The very next day she'd had her other visitor. Full of curiosity, she'd hurried down to the big reception room, gloomy and dark, despite its stridently gay purple, red and white paint. Nelson. And he had really thinned down.

He had also looked scared. "Let's get out of here. That old dragon at the door thinks I'm the rat who done you wrong. I know she does."

Tired as she was—Samantha had been awake all night again—she had felt suddenly young and carefree, her old self again. "Wait right here, and I'll bring down my daughter. You can come to the park with us."

He had been terrified of Samantha, that was clear, barely glancing in the big carriage that Dee and Roger had sent her. "Uh, lovely. Just like you. Except fatter."

"Speaking of fat, you look fantastic, Nelson. I can't believe it."

"Believe. And I owe it all to you. You made me think I could do it, and from there on in, it was a breeze. I'm lying. It was torture, but who cares. My parents are so happy they can barely stand it. In fact, all of us have decided Oaklon isn't such a bad hole. Listen, I'm the photographer for the yearbook. I've got all kinds of messages of you."

Waves of homesickness had washed over Alma as he brought her up to date on what was happening back at Oaklon Union High. How far away it seemed. She listened as Nelson told about the Senior Queen election.

Wilma had won, which figured. "And guess who's going to be her escort. No lie. I've taken her out the last two Saturdays."

"What a break for the poor girl." As they laughed,

Nelson had given her a scrutinizing look."You're different. Older? Better? Prettier, for sure."

"Wiser." And sadder, knowing that never again would a school dance be more than a childish memory. She was about twenty years older than Nelson, now.

"Also, I must point out, you look completely done in. Pretty rough, being the little mother?"

"No, no. I love taking care of her." But she hated the depression that seized her after he had left. She took Samantha back to the nursery, thinking about the bottles to sterilize, the laundry to do, homework—the big weekly therapy session was tonight; that would go on for hours. She had wondered why she lied so to everybody. It was rough. When she had to leave this place, it would be worse. She had it easy now, and maybe so did Samantha. She had started cramming wearily for her history final, but it was hard keeping her mind on World Wars I and II.

Samantha woke up, anyway, and for hour after hour had cried and fussed. Nothing had done any good. Alma had checked for open safety pins, changed her, offered her milk, water—had walked her up and down, patting her back.

For hours she had walked, as she did almost every night, with the sobbing baby in her arms, trying not to think of the daytime when Samantha cried, and she wasn't there. *"Set there forty minutes listening to that baby cry."* But she was doing all she could for her. Why did she have to cry so much!

"Stop it, Samantha. Stop it, *please, please, stop CRYING, STOP!"* She realized she had been shouting, actually shouting at her helpless baby, and she had burst into tears herself. Samantha cried on and on, until finally they both fell asleep in the chair. Alma

woke up cramped and weary, but at least Samantha
was fast asleep.

She knew then what she would have to do; slowly,
she took a page from her binder and sat down to write
Howard. From the beginning she had known she would
need his consent when she did this.

She discussed it quite a lot, with the therapy group
as well as with her social worker, but she hadn't phoned
Dee until she got Howard's reply a few days later,
through a lawyer; it had been a stiff and formal message; she had expected that. She had lied to him, but
Samantha owed her life to that deception, so she
couldn't regret it.

Roger and Dee had driven up the very next day, and
she had told them her decision. She was so tired she
couldn't keep the tears back. Roger's eyes had filled,
too, but Dee hadn't given in. She wouldn't allow herself to do that.

"It's the best thing to do. You tried, you gave it all
you had, and now you know it isn't going to be
enough."

"Not for her. Samantha's got to have the best. If I
wasn't always so tired and rushed . . . a baby should
have happy people around. Maybe that's why she
hasn't smiled yet. She's waiting until there's something
to smile about." That was so silly it had made them
laugh, she and Dee, a little hysterically. Even Roger
had smiled bashfully, mopping his eyes with his big
handkerchief. It wouldn't be fair to him to take on this
child, and Dee was fair. She would never ask him.

"I'm proud of you," Dee said simply. "You had the
guts, if you'll pardon my French, to have this baby in
the first place, and now you have the guts to give her

up. She'll never know how she lucked out when it comes to mothers." Dee hadn't given Samantha, now cooing in her crib, another glance. She had known she wouldn't ever see her again, her namesake grandchild. . . . Dee was tough enough to cut her losses.

It was Alma's turn to be tough now. She picked up the giant stuffed panda that Charlie had sent and put it in Samantha's basket. Maybe her new parents would let her keep it. They were coming for her at three. Alma had wanted the baby to leave before she did.

Samantha was going to a good home, the best home a baby could have. In general terms, the social worker had described them to Alma; her new father was a teacher, and—this was important—he wanted a baby just as much as her new mother did. They lived in a house with a big yard, a collie dog and a three-year-old brother. The mother had been a nursery school teacher, which was what Alma was going to be. She'd work with little children, like Bobby. Like Samantha would be, someday.

She took from the drawer the lacy little yellow dress, bonnet and booties that Wilma and Dilly had sent. Samantha had never yet had this set on. She'd been saving it for a special occasion.

This was special, all right. "Come on, darling. It's time to go." Gently, she lifted the sleeping baby onto her lap. Samantha was getting so heavy; in her sleep she made one of her soft little sounds, and Alma had to hug her close. It was a moment before she could go on with the dressing. For the last time she slipped off the little vest and gently pulled a clean one over the baby's downy pink head. Her eyes blurred, so it was hard to do up the tiny buttons on the yoke of the dress.

Her diaper was bone dry, but Alma changed her anyway, this last time.

She looked so beautiful. She was going to be very happy. Alma remembered again that social worker in Delesto: *Will come to see she doesn't need this baby for her emotional fulfillment.* Carefully, she tied the soft yellow booties on Samantha's exquisite little feet. That woman didn't understand how it was at all. It wasn't a question of her own need. It was right that Samantha should have a real family with a mother and father who both loved her. She had to have that. But just the same, on a deeper, more basic level, it was still wrong, wrong, for her and her baby to be parted. It was unnatural, a violence done—an arm being parted from a body. "Emotional needs" didn't come into it. But that was something Alma could never have explained to anybody.

"There you are, sweetheart." She tied the yellow satin bonnet ribbons around Samantha's fat chin. In the light the fine hairs on her head glinted. She was going to be a blonde, with Dee's dark eyes. "You'll wow them." Alma kissed each silky cheek, breathing in the smell of baby powder. "You're going to be so happy." She'd have a new name and never know about the time she was Samantha, and Alma was her mother. "Oh, they'll love you so much."

She hoped urgently that Dee and Roger would be on time. She didn't want to be alone in this room any longer than she had to, after she took Samantha down to the nursery. She wrapped her in her big white shawl, picked up the basket, started for the door and then had to come back. She sat down and rocked the baby to her. But it was three o'clock. She had to take her down.

Alma went to the door again, the baby warm and solid against her, but already her arms ached with vacancy. She memorized the soft brush of lashes, the sleeping little face; Samantha opened her eyes and, as if thinking of a joyous journey ahead, for the first time smiled, widely and unmistakably.

ABOUT THE AUTHOR

LAUREL TRIVELPIECE is the author of another
young adult novel, *During Water Peaches,* as
well as an adult suspense novel and a collection
of poetry. Her short stories and poems have
appeared in several leading literary magazines.

Ms. Trivelpiece is a graduate of the University
of California at Berkeley. She has two sons
and currently lives in Corte Madera, California.